Luck to Me

Stone Lake Series

Kaitlyn Richardson

Contents

Title Page   1

Epigraph   2

1. Hudson   3

2. Delilah   10

3. Hudson   20

4. Hudson   30

5. Delilah   39

6. Delilah   47

7. Delilah   55

8. Hudson   60

9. Delilah   76

10. Delilah   88

11.	Hudson	105
12.	Hudson	116
13.	Delilah	129
14.	Delilah	136
15.	Hudson	144
16.	Delilah	149
17.	Hudson	157
18.	Delilah	172
19.	Hudson	188
20.	Hudson	204
21.	Delilah	213
22.	Hudson	224
23.	Delilah	237
24.	Delilah	250
25.	Hudson	258
26.	Hudson	261
27.	Delilah	277
28.	Delilah	286
29.	Hudson	297

30. Hudson   303

31. Delilah   318

32. Delilah   325

Epilogue   338

Luck to Me

Stone Lake Series

Kaitlyn Richardson

"Had I not created my whole world, I would certainly have died in other people's."

-Anaïs Nin

Chapter One

Hudson

I 've been in love with Delilah Walton for eighteen years. Since the first day I stepped onto her family's farm.

At eight years old, I knew she would plague my mind for the rest of my days.

My dad was starting a new job as a ranch hand, and he took me with him. We drove through miles of emerald fields to get to a small town called Stone Lake, nestled in the northern part of the country. We drove and drove, only stopping once we reached a big white farmhouse with a wrap-around porch.

I had seen houses like this on the Saturday morning programs, but never in my life did I expect to be standing in front of one.

My dad and I may have been living in a ranching town now, but we lived in a small trailer on the outskirts of town. Nothing

3

compared to the endless fields and mansion-sized house in front of me.

The house here had an endless landscape around it. Our house was so close to the next that we could see into their windows.

The screen door screeched open, and out walked a man not much older than my father. He wore jeans and a button-down paired with cowboy boots and a hat. His face was leathery from the sun, but he greeted us with a happy smile.

"Welcome to Walton Ranch," he said while jutting his hand out to my father. My dad gave a gruff acknowledgment and shook his hand.

They started talking, but I wasn't listening, too busy looking at everything around me.

A young girl came flying out of a fenced-in garden near the house. Her little bare feet were pounding against the gravel.

She ran right up to the man, declaring, "We're having carrots for dinner!" Then lifted a hefty bundle of carrots up towards his line of sight.

The girl was wearing a red polka dot dress, covered in dirt. There were also a few dark streaks across her forehead and chin. Her cheeks were pink from the sun, and her crystalline blue eyes twinkled with unadulterated joy.

"Hudson, this is my daughter Delilah. She's a couple of years younger than you, but one of my sons is your age. My other boys are a few years older. I'm sure they'll all be pleased to have a new friend around here."

I gave a brief, pleasant greeting to Delilah, but that didn't seem to satisfy her.

She wrapped her delicate little hand around my wrists and started to tug. "Come on, Hudson! You're my best friend now!"

Then she pulled me into her side and we ran into the fields.

Her declaration that day still holds true. We are still friends, but I'm man enough to admit that I fell a little bit in love with her that first day, and my love has only grown since.

Not that I'd ever act on it.

Her brothers would tear me limb from limb.

It's an unspoken rule that you don't go after your friends' sister, which leaves me in a less-than-ideal situation.

The woman I *know* is the other half of my soul is off limits.

I'm teased daily by the nearness of her.

Forced to hear her gingle bell laugh. Forced to smell her fruity scent. Forced to watch her smile for people who aren't me.

The sun is just now rising over the horizon, casting the dark blue hue out and replacing it with a soft yellow.

A dew still decorates the field at my feet, but in mere hours, the sun will be blanketing us in piercing heat. Spring is fickle that way. Mornings and evenings are cool and damp, but for a few hours when the sun reaches its peak, the fields turn stifling.

I showed up at the ranch this morning and went to the barn to get my horse tacked up for chores. There was a note resting on my saddle telling me to head to the west field.

The steers are currently grazing in that field, but it's time to move them to another so they have access to fresh grass to graze.

Beckett, Delilah's oldest brother, is in charge of the ranch and everything it entails. He could send the ranch hands to drive the steers to a new field, but he always has the family do it instead.

Myself, Delilah, and her brothers Beckett, Cashton, and Emmett will be doing the drive by ourselves. My friend and her other brother, Henley, lives in the city. He's a hotshot hockey player, but he still comes home as often as he can. However, he *was conveniently unable* to come home for the drive.

Everyone is on their horses in the field, waiting, by the time I arrive.

"How kind of you to finally grace us with your presence," Delilah quips.

I shoot a glance at her. "Wanted to avoid seeing you for as long as possible."

That's a lie. I could look at her for the rest of my life and never get bored.

Through our friendship, we've adopted a relationship full of teasing and taunting. Not the type of teasing I'd like to do to Del, but I'll take anything I can get.

I had to find a way to be around her without embarrassing myself, so this is what I settled on. "At least the steers don't run when they see my face." No creature on the planet would.

"No, they probably mistake you for their own kind."

She huffs like I've offended her, even though she once showed me a photo of a pot-bellied hog and asked if it was my mother. Little thing has no restraint. It's one of the things I like most about her.

"Enough," Beckett declares. "Let's get this over with."

"Always the Scrooge, Beck." Del mumbles, and we all fight our laughter. He is an oddly grumpy guy and we love to give him shit about it. He never takes the bait, which only makes us try harder.

We all take off and start herding the steers through the fields.

It's nearing midday by the time we reach the dreaded river.

The Walton family farm is hundreds of acres of fields and woods, but a river splits the southern quadrant.

We spent countless hours here as children, swimming, fishing, and using a rope swing to cannonball into the water.

Crossing with a herd of cattle is, however, less than enjoyable.

The cows hate the water. They try to run out of the group to avoid it. The best cutter in the world would have a hard time keeping them together.

We push them in close. Each steer hugging another.

As soon as the first steer's hooves touch the water, we have problems.

It rears back, causing all the other to do the same. They start emitting mournful noises to show their discomfort.

We keep pushing, and the majority cross with only minor protest.

Two took off that we weren't able to stop. It was impossible to catch them without losing our hold on the herd.

Once we've successfully crossed the river, Becket points in my direction. "You and Del are on retrieval. Find the two we lost and bring them to the southern field."

With that, he, Cashton, and Emmett continue herding the steers the rest of the way. They only have a short distance left with no interruptions until they reach the field.

Del looks at me over her shoulder. Her hair is softly braided down her spine, and a hat rests atop her head. "Each steer is a point. Whoever gets the most wins."

Then she clicks her heels and her horse takes off.

With the primal urge to keep her close, I take off after her.

Chapter Two

Delilah

Being around Hudson is a paradox. I love him. I hate him.
I think I hate that I love him.

I'm not supposed to love him.

He certainly doesn't love me.

It's all so difficult.

I don't actually hate him, but the only way I can handle being around him is to pretend.

If I didn't, I'd make a complete fool of myself.

I'd happily stay in the friend zone for the rest of my life if it means I get to be around him.

So that's exactly what I do.

I pretend to hate him when I want to hold him. Pretend to loathe him when I know I love him.

It's worked as long as I've known him. And it will continue to work.

It has to.

Maybe my love for him is completely platonic. That's how it started. Then, as we got older, I began to wonder what more would feel like. Perhaps it was simply curiosity, rather than genuine feelings.

At least that's what I tell myself.

I left him at the river and headed for the woods, desperate for a moment's reprieve.

I ride my horse, Izarra, through the woods often, so she's used to the terrain. She has an inky black coat with a diamond-shaped white splash on her forehead.

My house is decently far from my family's farm, but if I cut through the woods, I can be there in half an hour. Izarra and I make the trek almost every day, so I'm confident in her ability to navigate the woods, despite the loose limbs and roots.

I search the river's edge until it meets the woods, but have no luck finding either steer.

I decide the only place left for them to be is in the woods.

If I were trying to hide, that's where I'd go.

We've been searching all day. The sun is starting to lower, making its great escape until tomorrow.

Hudson and I ran into each other about an hour ago, and neither one of us had any sightings yet. It's usually easy to find a runaway, but not this time.

The orange globe emits beams of light through the dark forest, casting eerie shadows.

The scent of pine lingers in the air, filling my lungs with an earthy aroma.

I feel so calm in the woods. Like nothing can touch me here.

A branch snaps a few feet away from me, and I spin in my saddle to see Hudson walking towards me.

"Any luck?" He has a sly grin that's far too mischievous to ignore.

"Does it look like I've had any luck?" I snap. Most of the time, I'm not actually frustrated with him. I'm frustrated that I have to play pretend.

But right now, knowing there's a competition on the line, I'm on edge.

I do not want to lose to him. He'll never let me live it down.

"No, it doesn't," he coos.

I throw up my hands, exasperated with him. "I'm fine here. Just go back to the safety of the fields."

He laughs, low and deep, spurring a purr in my chest.

"I just found you out of courtesy to let you know the score is one to zero."

WHAT! No, no, no!

I swing my leg over the saddle and drop to the ground, and march straight over to him.

He's wearing such a smug face.

"Tell me you're joking." It comes out like a plea. Even though the goal is to find both cows, I want to be the one to find them.

"Found the big guy on the edge of the woods about half an hour ago. Spent a few minutes patting myself on the back before I decided I should let you know the good news."

It is good news because we need to find them and bring them to the right field, but it means I'm losing the game.

The game I came up with!

"I will find the other one."

That makes him smile. His real smile. The one where his cheeks get round and scrunch his eyes at the corners.

"Why don't I walk with you. Clearly, you need the help."

I absolutely do not need help. I let him know just how I feel by rolling my eyes at him, spinning on my heel, and taking off in the opposite direction.

I grab Izarra's reins and wrap the thin leather around my palm. I know Hudson is going to follow me; he's always close by. That's why I don't bother mounting.

We walk in silence for a few minutes, heading deeper into the woods.

At some point, he advances in front of me. He holds all of the branches so they don't swing back and hit me in the face. He even offers to hold on to the reins so I can focus on looking for the steer.

The statement may be construed as mocking, but deep inside, I feel that he's sincere. Maybe it's wishful thinking.

Either way, I decline.

He shakes his head at me but continues on.

At this point, the sun has vanished. We are blanketed in a rich noir. The crickets are singing around us, and a chill is settling into the air.

The days have been stifling, but the nights are a reset.

It would be warmer in the fields right now. They prepare for the chill by holding hands with the sun all day. The woods block out the sun, having little to hold on to in the evenings.

A dusting of goose bumps prickles my flesh, but I continue moving forward.

Hudson doesn't seem bothered by the newfound cold. He's a big guy. Always has been.

He's always been taller than my brothers, and the more time he spent on the ranch, the bigger he got.

All ranchers are strong from the physical labor they do, but Hudson takes it to a whole new level.

His muscles put any others to shame.

No, he's not chilled because he has layer upon layer of thick, sexy muscle to keep him warm.

All I have is a button-down. It's cute, white with little blue stars, but not warm enough for a night in the forest.

"I think we need to start heading back, Del."

I look up and see nothing but inky black. The tree tops are blending in with the sky, blanketing us in.

"Fine," I say gruffly.

I hate to admit defeat, but we can't be walking around all night. We have to get back to the field and check on Hudson's horse anyway. Lucky's not as well-versed in the woods as Izarra is, so Hudson opted to leave him in the field.

"This does not mean you won," I say sternly, breezing past him. I don't want to look at his dumb, handsome face anymore.

"Maybe not won, but definitely winning."

Ugh. What a smug bastard.

"Just so you know," I start, my legs picking up speed. I'm feeling annoyed and want to get back "I will find it and once I do-"

My words get cut off as a sharp pain engulfs my ankle.

My brain goes fuzzy for a moment, but I swear I hear myself whimper.

I hit the cold, damp dirt beneath me. My wrists and palms sting from the impact, but the throbbing in my ankle is impossible to ignore.

It feels like the time Hudson, my brother Henely, and I were climbing the big oak tree on the property. We were having a competition to see who could get the highest.

The boys had a massive advantage over me. They were taller and stronger.

As a little girl, I was the smallest on the playground. Not much changed as I grew up. I'm still short with absolutely no muscle, but I've found a way to make it work for me.

The boys had already neared the top of the tree while I was only a few feet above the ground.

The branches were too thick for my hands, and I slipped and fell right to the ground.

I heard a crunch right before a blinding pain consumed me.

Hudson was there in a heartbeat, looking down at me with concern.

Very reminiscent of what he's doing now.

Except now, the pain in my ankle is masked by the butterflies in my stomach.

He's crouched down next to me, looking at me with concern and... is that fear?

His rough hands cradle my face. "Del, what happened? Are you okay?"

I try to open my mouth to speak, but all that comes out is a grumble.

I didn't hear a snap this time. When I fell from the tree, I broke my ankle.

The pain of a broken ankle was excruciating. The pain I'm feeling now was momentarily blinding, but nothing close to the pain before.

Hudson's eyes bore into me, pleading with me to answer him. One of his hands is trailing up and down my side, while the other is cradling my cheek.

His thumb delicately swipes underneath my eye, and I realize I'm crying.

"I'm fine. I think I just twisted my ankle."

Relief flashes through his eyes, but he doesn't take his hand off me. They continue to draw calming strokes.

Having him look at me with those dark eyes is too much for me. "I'm going to stand up now."

He moves back so I have room to stand up. I swing to my knees and feel the damp earth beneath me bleed through my jeans.

He holds his hand out for me to use for balance.

I try not to savor the way his hands absorb mine.

Starting to stand up with my good leg, I put pressure on my twisted ankle and tumbled forward, crying out.

Hudson is there, stopping me from falling by pulling me into his chest.

One of my hands is grabbing his bicep for stability, and the other is right above his heart. I feel it beating in rapid succession.

My ankle is screaming at me for attempting to stand. I didn't think it was this bad, but there's no way I'll be able to walk, let alone ride.

Hudson must see the conflict in my eyes because he picks me up under my knees and lifts me into the air.

"I'm fine, Hudson!" I smack his chest. I'm not fine, but I don't want him holding me like this. It's too hard not to envision us in a different situation. One where he wants me pressed against him. Not because I physically cannot hold myself up. "I can walk! Put me down!"

"Shut up, Del." His arms tighten, and I press even closer into him.

He smells like leather and pine. His scent is stronger than the forest around us, and I find myself leaning even closer.

I succumb to the temptation that is Hudson and lay my head against his chest.

I feel him tense and immediately pull away. That was stupid and impulsive. I don't need him teasing me over this. Or worse, telling my brothers. I would never live it down.

But he doesn't tease me. Instead, he takes the hand that's holding my shoulder and moves it up to my head, lightly pressing down until I'm once again resting against his chest.

His heart is pounding rapidly, to the beat of the cricket's song.

Where he's clearly on edge about the situation, I feel nothing but comfort. Sure, my ankle has its own heartbeat, but I'm at ease in his arms.

I let the warmth of him soothe me and allow him to carry me. Staying silent so as not to break this moment.

Chapter Three

Hudson

When she went down, my heart stopped.

It was like watching an angel fall from grace. Because that's what she is to me—an angel.

The moment she put pressure on her foot, I knew she was hurt worse than she let on.

I saw the way her eyebrows pulled together. How her chest rose and fell with low, shallow breaths.

She was trying to mask her pain, but I know her well enough to know when something's wrong.

I just didn't realize how bad it truly was.

Years of maintaining a respectful distance have made me a master of observation. I can read her face and know what she's feeling before she's even decided for herself.

And her face was telling me she was in pain.

It was instinctual to catch her as she fell. I would have reached for anyone going down. But I wouldn't be holding anyone else as tight as I am Del.

No. I would have helped them regain their balance and moved along.

Not with her.

I have her pressed tight against my chest. Her head cradled close to my neck.

She's curled in on herself, making herself fit against me like a puzzle piece.

My heart starts beating rapidly, and I'm certain she can feel it. My blood is racing so fast in my veins that I'm starting to feel lightheaded.

Her pear and honey scent wafts through the air, tickling my nose. The temptation is too great. I tip my nose to the crown of her head and take a deep inhale.

The loose tendrils of her dove colored hair brush my face, and I fight the urge to nuzzle closer.

She tilts her head up and meets my eyes. The glow of the moon illuminates her blue irises, creating an otherworldly shine.

They glisten with unshed tears that she is refusing to let fall. I know she's in pain, but she will refuse to tell me.

"You can put me down now. I can walk just fine." Her voice is soft when she speaks. She knows as well as I do that she can't walk. She just can't put her pride aside.

"Maybe I just like you in my arms." I try to sound teasing, but my words are nothing but truthful.

Her eyes soften. She's allowing herself to imagine a scenario where my words are real. Then they steel back to fierce. "Probably as much as I like being in them," she huffs out.

I hit her with my best smirk and fire back, "I've never had complaints. All the women in my arms are always begging for more."

She sticks a finger in her mouth and makes a fake gagging sound.

I can't help but laugh at her gesture. She's never been one to shy away from sharing her opinions.

"I'd rather eat a lollipop off the barn floor than hear about your conquests, Hudson."

"If you're jealous, just say so." That's going to drive her crazy.

She starts to wiggle and gives me a smack on my chest.

I was right.

She did not like that.

"I have no trouble finding someone to share my bed with. I don't need to slum it with you."

Now I'm pissed.

I don't like the idea of someone touching her. I want her all to myself. She better not give me names because there's no way I could walk past them and not punch them square in the nose.

I've always been that way with her. Hating the guys she's hanging around. They're never good enough for her.

I hate the way they're always so casual with her.

She's a prize, and they should treat her as such.

If I could eradicate all men, I would. Simply for the fact that I don't like them around her.

I feel my muscles in my shoulders stiffen. Even thinking about her with a man makes me see red.

She's not mine. I have no claim over her. Yet, I hate the idea of her not being mine.

I've always been her protector. Growing up as her brother's best friend, I learned to watch after her.

When they were giving her a hard time, I was on her side. When kids at school were picking on her, I was her supporter. When she started going on dates in high school, I was the one who let the boys know there would be repercussions for hurting her.

Of course, her brothers were always looking after her too. As the girl with four brothers, the boys learned quickly not to mess with her.

Some were foolish enough to hurt her and met my fist as penance. Always met with approval from her brothers.

They never thought of my disapproval of her dating as anything more than brotherly concern. If they knew I hated it because I wanted to be the one going out with her, they'd hang, draw, and court me.

The moon has taken center stage in the sky, surrounded by a blanket of stars. The crickets are the only noise around us besides the occasional frog from the river and the mush of damp leaves underfoot.

After the trek through the woods, I step into an open grazing field, Delilah still in my arms.

We're going to have to spend the night out here. Her ankle is too hurt to ride, and we're too far to walk. We're safe in this field from predators. Their entire property is fenced in.

"We're staying here tonight. We can head back and find the steers in the morning."

I lower her to the ground, making sure to keep her ankle elevated.

"We can ride back. No need to be dramatic."

"Your ankle is so fat it won't fit in the stirrup," I point out, and even in the darkness, I can see a blush paint her cheeks.

I leave her sitting in the grass to tie up Izarra next to Lucky. They give a few huffs but will be content spending the night out here. They are very familiar with each other, so I don't worry about them.

"Hey! Where's the steer you found?" She shoots from her spot a few feet away.

I knew she would bring this up.

"I lied," I yell back over my shoulder.

"I knew it!" I hear her triumphantly whisper to herself.

I feel myself grinning. I knew that would make her happy.

Double-checking that both of their leather bridles are secured, I give them each a gentle pet before walking back to Del.

She has her knees pulled up to her chest and is shivering. Her little body is practically vibrating from her chills. She wasn't cold at all when I was holding her, and smugly, that feels good.

I sit down next to her and immediately feel the dew on the grass bleed through my jeans. It won't be comfortable, but it certainly won't be the worst place I've spent the night.

I've spent plenty of nights in the fields surrounding the farm, and I know Delilah enjoys spending nights out under the stars.

She's resting her chin on her knees, snugged up in a tight ball.

All of the heat of the day has disappeared, leaving a crisp blanket over us.

I don't feel cold, but Del is clearly freezing. I shrug out of my Detroit jacket and sling it over her shoulders.

She wiggles to get her arms in the sleeves and whispers, "Thank you." I feel an odd sense of accomplishment knowing I'm providing her warmth.

She looks so good swimming in my jacket.

I lie back and take in the stars overhead.

After a few beats, Delilah copies my move and lies down next to me. We are so close that our legs and arms touch.

I feel her warmth seeping into my exposed arms. She's so close I can smell her sweet scent.

I'm about to open my mouth and ask if she's doing okay, but she beats me to it and says, "Tomorrow we're finding those steers. I refuse to ask my brothers for help."

"But you don't mind asking mine?"

She waits a few beats, chewing on her bottom lip. "They would help me just to prove I need it. You would help me simply because you know it would ease my troubles."

I'm left tongue-tied. She doesn't get deep very often. Don't get me wrong, she's not afraid of emotion. She just tends to lean more towards lighter conversations.

"I'll always help you, Del. With anything you need." And I mean that. I'll always be here for her.

We watch the stars for a while, each pointing out new shapes. Her arm raises towards the heavens, drawing the patterns so I can see them.

After some time, her arm falls down to her side, and her breathing evens out. I quietly move my head to the side to look at her. Her delicate button nose is pointing to the sky, her dark lashes resting against her rosy cheeks. Her lips are parted slightly, and she snores lightly.

She is so beautiful.

Lying here in the grass with her reminds me of doing this as children. She's always lived in the moment. Doing what she loved, when she loved it. She's never feared judgment, which she often receives.

Although we grew up together, our childhoods were very different.

When my father started working at the farm, I experienced moments of childlike happiness that I had never had before.

Delilah and her family gave me moments that made my life feel like a movie.

At some point, I drift off, letting the evening breeze carry me to sleep, along with the gentle whispers of Del's breathing.

Not long later, I'm startled awake by a pressure on my chest. I open my eyes and see that Delilah has snuggled up to my side, draping an arm over my chest and a leg over my own. She nuzzles her cheek into my sternum before she settles.

My chest tightens in response. I've dreamed about what this moment might feel like, and now that it's happening, I never want it to end.

I brush a whisp of brown hair off her face and tuck it behind her ear, tracing my fingers down her face. My other hand rests on her shoulder, and I use the angle to pull her closer to me.

Her heat feels like the sunshine of a July afternoon. Sitting by the lake, grilling wieners with friends. A beer in one hand, a hand of cards in the other. She reminds me of the happiest times.

I watch her for a while, cementing this moment in my memory. Her hair drifting in the breeze, her chest rising and falling in a calming rhythm. Her cheeks are flushed from being wrapped in my jacket and snuggled into my chest.

I should extract myself from her. I'm teasing myself by allowing this situation to continue. If I could stop time right now and freeze her to me, I would.

I fight my drooping eyes for as long as I can, but when I finally succumb to sleep, I dream of more moments exactly like this.

Chapter Four

Hudson

12 Years Old

*M*y *dad and I have worked out a routine for the work he's supposed to do on the ranch.*

He doesn't do anything, and I pick up the remains. In other words, I do his job and he takes the money.

The bar in downtown has a pool hall that he goes to every night. He spends the entire night there. Playing cards, playing pool, watching races.

All of his favorite forms of gambling.

And of course, you can't gamble your night away without drinking. I don't know what he spends more money on: his bets or his booze.

We have our own house, a trailer on the edge of town. It's all the space the two of us need, so I don't complain, but we don't spend much time there. The Waltons have a bunkhouse for all the workers to stay in, which we use most of the time.

Well, my dad does. I usually stay in the big house with Henely, Beckett, Cashton, and Emmett. Well, Delilah's there too, but her brothers don't like it when she tags along much. She's only ten, and they say she can't keep up with us. I don't mind having her around. She's funny, and I think she keeps up just fine.

My dad was too tired this morning to do the fence round he's assigned to, so I had to get up early and do it. He's supposed to ride the perimeter of the ranch and make sure all the fences are intact.

I got up early this morning, hoping to get his work done quickly so I could go to the river with the guys. They found a rope tied to a tree that hangs over the water, and we are going to swing from it and drop in.

My hope is squandered when I find a broken fence post in the east field.

I swing off the horse I'm using to assess the damage. There are several horses that the ranch hands can use, and since I don't have my own, like the guys, I have to borrow one.

It looks like an easy fix, so I pull a wrench out of my saddle bag and start pulling the broken wires back together.

I hear hoof beats in the distance, and look over my shoulder to see Mr. Walton riding up on his horse.

"Hi, Mr. Walton!" I shout, hoping he can hear me over his horse's feet pummelling the ground.

He's wearing his signature cowboy hat. I've never seen him without it on. Even when he's done for the day and eating dinner, he keeps it on.

He comes to a stop beside me, so I push myself up from a crouch and walk up to him, giving his horse a scratch when I get close enough.

"What are you doing out here? All the boys rode down to the river."

Damnit. I wasn't fast enough. Hopefully, they'll go again and I'll get my dad's work done before they leave next time.

I try to hide my disappointment and answer. "Was just doing fence patrol. Found a broken one, so I'm trying to fix it quickly."

He assess me. Eyes drawing up and down my body. I wonder if he notices the rip in my knees or the tear in my elbow. Or the fact that my sneakers are too small. He probably notices my shoes, not that they're too small, but that they aren't cowboy boots. It's hard to do much on a ranch without any, but I don't have a pair, so I make it work. If he does notice, he doesn't say anything about it.

"I see what you're doing. I'm just wondering why? I pay your father to do this, not you."

Crap. I don't want him to fire Dad. If he loses this job, he'll most likely move us again. I love this ranch and all my friends. Even though I'm just a ranch hand's kid, they let me pretend I'm part of the family. They let me eat dinner in the big house with them. They let me ride their horses whenever I want. They take me to watch Henely's hockey games when he plays in the next town over. I don't want to lose any of it.

"Dad's not feeling well today, so I thought I'd help out." I try to sound nonchalant, like it's no big deal, but Mr. Walton is looking at me like he knows a secret.

"I bet I know exactly what's got him feeling under the weather," he murmurs under his breath.

I don't say anything. If he didn't know before, he does now. I don't want to confirm it, so I just let the silence flow.

"Go catch up with the boys," he commands while flinging an arm in the direction of the river.

"I gotta finish this first." Then I turn back to the fence. As long as the work gets done, it doesn't matter who does it. Right?

"Go," he commands. "I've got it from here."

He swings off his horse and heads to the stump post, pulling the wrench out of my hand.

"It's no trouble, really." I don't want anything to happen to Dad, or Mr. Walton to be upset with me.

"Boy, get out of here and be a kid for once." Then he starts working on the fence, effectively dismissing me.

Later that night, after an afternoon of swimming in the river and drinking beer we stole from one of the ranch hands, I'm sound asleep on the couch of the big house.

Henely, Emmett, Cashton, and Beckett are asleep in their rooms upstairs. I saw Delilah sneak in through the porch door a few hours ago. I always wonder what she gets up to when there's no one around. She's probably working in her garden or simply watching the stars. We climbed onto the roof one night while her brothers were out of town. She showed me all the shapes in the sky called constellations.

The silence of the house is interrupted by the twisting of a doorknob and a quick rush of air as the door is pushed open. Whoever it is, they are careful not to let the handle slam into the wall.

Everyone who lives here is long asleep, so I know it's none of them, but I know exactly who it is.

"Hudson, you in here?" My dad is peering around the hallway entrance, trying to see me in the dark.

I want to slink deeper into the couch cushions and hide under the quilted blanket that their mother made. I want to ignore him. I want him to go away.

"Boy! I see you," he says sharply.

My heart starts beating rapidly. I knew it was no use hoping. He'd search until he found me.

I get up from the safe haven of their couch and pull my discarded shirt back over my head, then walk over to the front door, not saying a word to my dad.

I crouch down and pull on my sneakers, then stand and wait for him to lead me outside.

We get in his rusted-out truck, careful to shut the doors quietly so no one wakes up and finds us.

We drive the twenty minutes to town in silence. What's there to say? I know the routine. This isn't a rare occurrence. It happens more days than it doesn't.

We park around the block and walk through the dark to The Prairie Pint Bar. *My dad swings the door open and immediately comes to life. "Gentleman," he cheers and makes his way to the bar top, leaving me standing by the entrance.*

A few of the regulars grace me with hellos, but I stay quiet. I know why I'm here. I walk past the dark, paneled walls, decorated with glowing signs, and head over to the pool tables.

Two games are going on, leaving the third table empty. Each table has a dim, stained glass light dangling over the middle, casting a moody glow over the area.

I pull a stool over to the wall and try to fight my yawns as I watch the games go on.

I'm running on just a few hours of sleep from getting up so early to cover for my dad. He functions better at night, which is why he's usually asleep during working hours. Since I have to cover his shift and accompany him to the bars, I get very little sleep, but I've learned how to function on it.

My shoulders ache from the sunburn I got at the river today, as I wait.

After about an hour, my dad is sufficiently liquored up and swaggers over to me. He slaps a hand on my shoulder in what may be mistaken as a loving gesture, but it's his way of letting me know that I need to start a game.

Ignoring the sting his hand left on my chapped shoulder, I rise and pick up my pool stick. I don't need to announce that I want to play; everyone is watching.

My dad's been dragging me to bars for years. I played once for fun and nailed every shot I took. From that point forward, I've been my dad's ace in the hole.

His game is to tell the surrounding patrons that his son's playing, so now's their easy chance to win. Little do they know that I never miss. Every bet my dad takes when I play wins him money.

Since we've been in this town longer than the rest, the regulars all know about the jig. Sometimes they play to try to beat me. Other times, on big rodeo weekends, my dad can play his regular trick and snake the out-of-towners out of their money.

Tonight, I play against a local who is so drunk he can't stand without swaying, let alone shoot a cue straight. I send all my balls into the pockets before he gets one.

I'm down to the eight ball, and Dad places a sizable bet that I'll land it in the corner pocket.

I used to feel pressure to make it where he bet. Now, I just want to get it over with.

I draw the stick back, take a steadying breath, and fire the cue into the right ball. A rhythmic clink sounds on contact, and the eight ball glides perfectly into the pocket.

The gathered crowd hoots and hollers as if they haven't seen this exact move three other times this week.

My dad collects his winnings and sets up another game for me to play. This process continues for a few more hours until the sun begins to peak over the horizon.

This late, my dad is so drunk that he can't walk straight. He's lost all his earnings and spent money he doesn't have on liquor.

With some convincing, I talk him into heading back to the ranch. I need to get back soon if I want to get his chores done on time.

I fix him into the passenger seat, struggling to get his much larger body situated. Then I hop into the driver's seat, fire up the engine, and head back to the farm.

Chapter Five

Delilah

I hear a loud, incessant ringing that jars me from the most peaceful night of sleep I've ever had. A blanket of warmth surrounds me, cocooning me in something heavy.

I crack open my eyes and come face to face with a dark surface. I can't determine what it is, but it's warm and smells like Hudson.

Wait...

I move my hand up the broad expanse and feel fields of hard muscles under my fingertips. I allow myself a moment to indulge in the feel of him before pushing myself up.

At some point during the night, I must have curled up next to him. Well, I more like wrapped myself around him. He's so warm. I'm so warm. I must have sought his heat during the night, and he did not disappoint.

The ringing continues, but it hasn't woken Hudson yet. He's still sound asleep beneath me. His lashes resting against the hard lines of his face, a light layer of stubble on his jaw. His lips are full, pushing out little clouds of air.

I move to stroke his face, hopefully to ease him out of sleep, but find my body pinned down. His thick arms, corded with muscles and dark tattoos, are wrapped tightly around my waist. He's holding on like he's afraid I'll blow away in the wind.

The air is cool on my cheeks, but I feel nothing but a calming warmth from being wrapped in Hudson's arms. The night sky is still among us, but it is hued with lavender streaks, an indication that the sun will soon be rising.

I want to pretend I'm still sleeping. Lay my head back against his chest and let his breathing lull me back to sleep.

Maybe he won't hear what I presume to be his phone ringing. It's probably just my brothers asking where we are. I don't have my phone with me; I left it in the barn, but they know we were together. They aren't worried about us being alone together, because nothing will ever happen between us. I'm certain they're just pissed that we never brought the loose steers back.

He starts to stir, so I push back slightly. I don't want him thinking I was crawling all over him last night.

His eyes pop open and immediately meet mine. His dark globes momentarily flash with a deep contentment, his arms still bound around my waist.

Then, he registers his surroundings.

In an instant, he releases his hold of me, pushes me off him, and shifts his body to a sitting position. He shifts his weight and pulls his phone out of his back pocket.

I try not to let the hurt of his rejection sting, but I fail miserably.

Without his heat, a layer of goosebumps appears on my skin.

He takes a quick second to look at the number on the screen before putting it up to his ear. He watches my face with intensity. He totally caught me holding onto him. But he was holding me back, so maybe he won't tease me too bad about it.

The conversation goes quickly. He does all the listening and doesn't say a word. I hear a muffled voice from the other end when he pulls the phone from his ear and hangs up, shoving it back in his pocket.

I attempt to ease the tension in the air. "Are my brothers threatening to kill you for spending the night with me?" My tone is flirtatious, but completely teasing. When we were teenagers, they started telling Hudson that he was never allowed to be near me romantically. I was effectively off limits. Since then, I tease him and he teases me right back.

He completely ignores my jab, which is very unlike him. He never misses a chance to torment me.

He looks around, dazed. He still looks half asleep, but jumps to his feet and walks away.

"Hey! Is everything okay?" He's acting weird. He wouldn't be this stressed over a stupid joke with my brothers. Maybe it's my brother, Henley? He and Hudson are only two years older than me and are thick as thieves. Even though Henley moved to the city to follow his hockey career, the two of them remained close. He'd tell me if it was him, right?

He walks right over to Lucky and unties his bridle from the tree. His horse is brown in the front and white in the butt, with little matching brown dots decorated across. He has a boring brown saddle and bridle. Not nearly as fun as my blue set. My brother Cashton made both of us nameplates. Hudson's saddle has a simple, metal plaque on the back that reads "Lucky," and I have a plaque with little stars that reads "Izarra." Cash works with metal professionally now, but started as a teenager making small trinkets.

"Hudson!" He's starting to piss me off by ignoring me. "What the hell is going on?"

The shrill in my voice has him looking over his shoulder at me, but he turns right back around and swings his leg up and over the saddle. He adjusts his position and clicks his heels in, causing Lucky to start moving.

"I'm sorry, Del. I have to go." Then he flicks his reins and rides off in the direction of the ranch.

"What about the steers?" I scream in his direction, but he's too far away to hear me. I watch him ride away until he disappears from view.

I cannot believe the douche lord left me here. What am I supposed to do now? Find the steers for starters, I suppose.

He should be here helping me. No matter how pissed I am at his spur of the moment disappearing act, I have to find them and bring them to their new home.

Finding them might prove to be a challenge, but once I do, getting them to the right field will be no problem. I grew up doing round-ups. I'm perfectly capable of driving them alone.

But just because I can do it, doesn't mean I want to. If Hudson had stuck around, it might not have been more fun, but at least it wouldn't have been as stressful. Having backup takes the pressure off.

He makes me so angry! Not so much as an explanation. Just shoves me away like a bad sardine and is on his way.

I feel cheap.

I know this wasn't some one-night stand where the guy can't even look me in the eyes when it's done. Yet, this stings worse. It's Hudson. The Hudson I care about and who means something to me.

Him abandoning me, like I mean nothing, hurts.

I allow myself fifteen seconds to pout, then get to business by planting my hands in the morning grass and letting the cool moisture of the dew wake me up further.

I push my body weight up and jump to a squatting position. I feel a tinge of pain in my bad ankle, but it can handle the pressure I'm putting on it.

Slowly standing, I test my weight on my ankle. I feel a few sharp pains, but am able to walk. Resting last night was the right call. It probably would've been much worse if I hadn't.

With a slight hobble, I walk the ten feet of grass separating me from the tree Izarra is tied to. I can't wait to get these boots off my feet. They've been on for twenty-four straight hours. Hopefully, just a few more to go.

Using my good ankle, I put a foot in the stirrup and get myself situated in the saddle.

"Good morning, my beauty," I whisper to my girl and give her a couple of scratches. She twitches her ears in response, letting me know she's ready to run.

I look for the steers until the sun rises and find them both quickly. At some point during the night, they must have found each other and decided to keep each other company.

They were standing together like Siamese twins by the river. The thing they were terrified of yesterday is no longer a concern. They idly sip the water from the stream and show no sign of distress when I start moving them across the moving water.

After a few miles of trekking through the fields, we come upon the other steer, and I release them to join their pack.

Screw Hudson.

I don't need him. He probably would have just slowed me down anyway.

Loser.

They all used to abandon me when we were children. Leaving me. Excluding me. Running away from the ranch and leaving me all alone.

Hudson was the only one who ever stuck up for me, which always makes it sting worse when he's the one who leaves me high and dry.

Chapter Six

Delilah

Much to my brother's dismay, I own my own business. Now, don't get me wrong, they're proud of me. They aren't the type to think a woman belongs hidden at home. In fact, I know they are beyond proud of me for being self-sufficient and finding my own way in the world.

Well, that fits the script for three out of the four. My oldest brother, Beckett, is proud of me, but wishes I would dedicate more of my time to the family farm.

It's rich coming from him, considering he lives and breathes the ranch.

Emmett spends most of his time away from home traveling on the rodeo circuit. My other brother, Cashton, makes his living as a fairer. And my youngest brother is a professional hockey player in the city.

We all pitch in at the ranch, but we also all have our own thing. Except for Beckett. After our parents died, he inherited everything.

He's dedicated his entire life to the ranch and our parents' legacy. Some days I worry that he has nothing that's truly his. That he only runs the place out of principle. Some days he seems truly miserable, but he won't even entertain a conversation about his feelings. He's a closed book.

My business is something that's entirely my own. Something that's not tied to anyone else. Something I enjoy doing that allows me to support myself.

When I was a kid, my mother taught me how to make jam. We would pick berries together in the far fields, load up five-gallon buckets worth, and drag them back home.

Our shoulders would be bright red from the sun, and our backs would be sore from hunching over the bushes for so long.

My dad would watch us walking up to the house with our full buckets and tell the boys to set up the tents in the yard.

The house always got extremely hot from canning, so Dad and the boys would go outside while my mom and I worked. They knew they would just get in our way. Not to mention the unbearable heat. Having the stove on for endless hours, combined with the summer heat, made the house unbearable to be in.

Mom and I would open all the windows, letting the curtains dance in the breeze. As the sun set, the house would cool down. We would work through the night until the morning chickadees started to sing. Then we made our way outside and curled up in the tents with my dad and brothers.

After she died, I made jam as a way to feel close to her. I would spend days collecting every type of berry I could find. Spend countless hours crafting new recipes. Spend days making the house feel like a sauna from the oven being perpetually used.

By the end of the first summer without her, I had enough jam to feed the entire town for a year. I gave jars as gifts, thank-yous, congratulations, and everything in between.

Everyone and their mothers got some of my jam. The entire town was using it on their morning toast.

It didn't take long before the retro diner in town tasted my creations and proposed a business deal. They wanted to buy my jam in bulk and serve it at the restaurant. Buy. With real money!

For a sixteen-year-old, the idea of making money was, of course, enticing.

In a matter of months, my jam became a must-have at the restaurant. I realized I had a real business on my hands.

The restaurant was placing larger and more frequent orders. I had a real source of income. Not that I needed it. I was just a teenager. I was living at home and going to school. I had no need for all the money I was making, but Beckett helped me set up an account that would hold all of my earnings until I was eighteen.

Since the jam was so popular at the busiest place in town, other businesses began requesting my jam, and the local grocery store even started carrying it.

I felt like a celebrity, with everyone in town knowing and loving what I was creating.

To this day, I spend my nights crafting new and unique flavors.

After I got home from finding and relocating the steers, I took a long bath in my claw-foot tub, cracking open my red and blue-stained glass window so the bird songs could offer their relaxing melody. I filled the water up to my collarbone and let the steam rise around me.

I added some lavender oil to the water to help relax my muscles. Sleeping on the hard ground has serious consequences, but the bath is helping to alleviate them.

After drying off and dressing in a comfortable pair of jean shorts and a white cami top, I throw my hair into a loose bun on top of my head and head to the kitchen.

While my tub was filling up, I started boiling down some blueberries. I came up with a new flavor combination and decided to test it tonight to see if it's worth making a bulk amount for sale.

The other week, I was over for dinner at the big house, and I was eating a bowl of homemade blueberry ice cream. Hudson was sitting next to me on the couch, eating a bowl of peaches. I harmlessly plucked one out of the bowl with my fingers and plopped it in my mouth. The flavors mixed so well that I was inspired to try them in a jam.

I only use fresh fruit in my jams, and peaches don't grow this far north. Luckily for me, a man from South Carolina drives up every few weeks and sells them out of his truck. A while ago, we made a deal that he would reserve several crates for me as long as I gave him a few jars of jam.

In my opinion, what makes my jam so unique, besides the fresh fruit used, is my secret sauce. In every batch of jam, I add a splash of liquor. Just a dash. Just enough to complement the existing flavors. It's what sets my jam apart from others.

I peel the peaches I picked up a few days ago, their juice dripping down to my wrists, and throw them into the boiling pot with the blueberries, adding some spices and a splash of bourbon.

The fruity scent and warming spices fill my little kitchen with a mouthwatering scent. After a few minutes, I dip a spoon into the fruit to get a taste.

The blueberries are tart, the peaches are sweet, and the spices and bourbon are warm. This jam is fantastic, but it's still not perfect.

I run over to my fridge and pull out a lemon. Yes! I need something with zest. The tangy flavor will complete the flavor palette.

I stir until the lemon is incorporated and give the jam another taste. I actually moan out loud when the flavors hit my tongue. This might be one of my best creations.

I only made enough for one jar, so I funnel it into a jar and stick it in my fridge. I'll have to plan a weekend away to pick a bunch of blueberries. I know a secret spot deep in the woods beyond town that has miles and miles of blueberry bushes.

With inspiration flowing through me, I clean up and decide to head to bed, slipping out of my shorts, tossing my covers back, and crawling into bed. I can hear the wind chimes outside my window and close my eyes to their gentle song.

It feels so lovely to be in a real bed instead of the cold, hard ground.

Great... I'm once again reminded of stupid Hudson and how he ditched me this morning.

The stupid jacket he let me wear last night is draped over the chair I have in the corner of my room, and I swear his smell is wafting off of it.

There better have been a damn good reason for him leaving me out there all alone. Part of me wants to tell my brothers he abandoned me in the field. They'd be way more upset than I am. They have some weird arrangement where they all feel the need to look after me. I don't need it, but they think I do. They'd act as if he left me in imminent danger.

Ridiculous, I know.

I'm not going to tell them because I don't want them mad at him. I'll just quietly stew until I can get him back for it.

I know deep down he had a good reason for what he did; otherwise, he never would have just left me there.

Great. Now I'm all riled up and don't feel tired at all.

I lay in bed for what feels like hours, shifting between being mad at Hudson and remembering how good it felt to have his arms holding me close to him.

After what feels like hours, I fall asleep to the thoughts of his warmth surrounding me and what would have happened if he hadn't left.

Chapter Seven

Delilah

Ten Years Old

I've been looking for a four-leaf clover for two years.

Not long after Hudson and his dad started hanging out at the farm, Mr. Owen told me all about four-leaf clovers. He told me they are a symbol of good luck and that having one will bring me fortune.

I wasn't sure what fortune meant, but a bit of luck would be nice. To me, it sounded more like a constant falling star. My mom and dad told me that falling stars bring luck and grant you a wish. It sounds like four-leaf clovers do that all the time, unlike having to wait for the stars to fall.

"What are you doing?" Hudson is standing right beside me, his body blocking the sun from my eyes. I'm on my knees in the middle of the field behind the barn. My dress has grass stains on the hem from kneeling in the dirt, looking for clovers all afternoon.

As soon as Mr. Owens finished telling me about the rare four-leaf clovers, I ran to the field I knew they grew in. I've been looking for hours but haven't found a single one yet. My mom tried to convince me to take a break and have some lunch, but I didn't want to give up.

I know he said they are rare, but I've looked through hundreds and haven't found a single one.

"I'm looking for a four-leaf clover." I don't bother looking at him when I tell him. I can't risk losing my place.

I feel him kneel down next to me, his knees hitting the ground in a section I haven't looked in yet. "Hudson!" I squeal and push his shoulder.

"Woah, what'd I do?" He looks a little panicked from my outburst, and he holds his hands out in front of himself.

"I haven't looked there yet, and now you're crushing a potential four-leaf clover."

His eyes grow wide, and he looks over his shoulder, scanning the field behind him. "You've searched this far into the field for a clover?" His tone is mixed with shock and disbelief.

"Yes, but no luck." I shrug as if it's no big deal, but I really, really, really want to find one.

I get back to searching, ignoring Hudson's presence. I like having him around; he's funny and nice—the total opposite of my jerk brothers. But I need to focus right now.

"Your mom told me dinner would be done in a few minutes. She's making hot dogs and grilled corn."

As if on cue, my belly rumbles. I put a hand over it to silence it, but it's too late.

"Tell her I'll be late, I have to keep looking." He's distracting me. I can't remember where I left off. I'll just start this section over. I don't want to risk missing one.

"You can always come back tomorrow," he says nonchalantly.

I could, but I want one now. I just shake my head and keep looking.

We're both quiet for a while, but he doesn't move to leave. Just stays kneeling beside me.

A few minutes pass, and I notice pink streaks starting to appear in the sky. The spring sky takes hours to set fully, but it will begin to gradually get darker over the next few hours.

I look behind me to see what Hudson is still doing here. He's holding his face inches from the ground. "What are you doing?"

He puts a finger down to mark his place and looks up at me. "I'm helping you find the clover." He smiles at me and gets back to work.

I smile to myself, feeling a burst of giddy energy, and start looking again, too.

My brothers would never help me find a four-leaf clover. They'd call me stupid and take the lawn mower to my field. Hudson's much nicer than they are. He doesn't call me names, and he helps me get the ice cream out of the carton when it's too frozen for me to scoop.

I'm glad my brothers are friends with him. I like when he's around. He tells me jokes before he tells anyone else, and he even lets me ride on the tractor that my parents told me I'm too young for.

My brothers call him one of their own, but he doesn't feel like a brother to me. He feels like a friend.

We keep looking in companionable silence until the orange starts to bleed into the sky, mixing with the cotton candy pink, and it's too dim to see the clovers properly.

I keep looking religiously every afternoon for the elusive four-leaf clover when I've finished my daily chores. But, I have no luck finding one. Maybe you need the luck of the clover to find said clover. Perhaps it's just one big loop of never finding one because you don't have any luck to start with.

Mr. Owen didn't say he had one, so maybe he was just making it up. Sometimes he talks in a funny way and says things that don't make sense, but I asked my parents if they were real, and they both told me they had seen one with their own eyes before, so I continued to look day after day.

A few times when I was checking on the horse, I peeked through the barn doors and saw Hudson all alone, crouched down in the clover field. I think he's looking for one too.

I hope he lets me see it if he finds one first. Maybe he'll even let me borrow it if I need some extra luck. I bet he would. He's always nice to me. I know I'd let him borrow my luck if he needed it.

Chapter Eight

Hudson

When I woke up, it felt as though I were still dreaming.

The warm pressure of her slender body snuggled under my arm was the closest I'll ever come to Shangri-La.

I've spent countless hours imagining how her body would feel pressed against mine. And now, I know.

I know that her head fits perfectly in the crook of my shoulder. I know that leg fits in between my own like a puzzle piece. I know that her breasts feel heavy when they're pressed against my chest.

It nearly killed me to pry myself off of her. I would have been content if my life ended in that moment because I would have departed as a contented man.

She was hurt when I ran so abruptly. Her big blue eyes were wide as saucers. Her lips parted in a gasp. Her eyebrows were pinched together in a way I know means she was hurt and confused.

I hate that I did that to her.

When I woke up, I felt a multitude of emotions at once. Complete and total ecstasy due to the girl I've wanted for years lying on top of me. Confusion because the aforementioned girl was lying on top of me. And finally, anger because my stupid phone ruined it.

Anyone who called and disturbed that moment would be on my shit list, but pulling my cell out of my pocket and seeing who was calling sent my mood from bad to worse.

My dad's name was written across the screen, and I knew. I knew he was in trouble and that I would have to bail him out. That's the way it's been since I was a child. He gets into trouble, and I have to clean up the mess. Neither of us outgrew this cycle as I aged from boy to man. He takes advantage of me, and I let him.

It's been the way we operate for as long as I can remember. He does whatever he wants with no regard for anyone else, and I'm left to deal with it.

I know I should hate him. Should leave him to drown in the water he's spilled. But I can't.

Maybe that makes me pathetic. That I'd abandon every-thing to run to his rescue.

But he's my dad.

I'm all he has, so it's my job to take care of him.

It was his phone that called me, but the voice on the other end was Timmy. He's the current bartender at the bar on the outskirts of town. That's where my dad spends his days and nights now. He's not allowed to enter the bar in town anymore, so he slums it on the outskirts.

Against my better judgment, I answered the phone.

The loud, grating voice of Timmy yelling in my ear shouts, "There's a problem at the bar, kid."

I didn't say anything back. Delilah was staring at me with the biggest doe eyes that caused my brain to short-circuit. In that moment, her scent still swimming around me, her heat still lingering on my body, I was overwhelmed.

I don't know how long I stared at her, but the voice came again. "Your dad's been here all night. I gotta get home. Come get him, or I'm leaving him for the cops to deal with."

That snapped me out of it.

He's had his fair share of run-ins with the police, but I do my best to keep that from happening. He does bad things, but he's not a bad man. He just needs a little help, which is what I'm there for. Even if I hate it.

"You coming or what, kid? I can't be waiting here all day for you to come get his no good-" I pull my phone away from my ear, hang up the phone, and shove it back in my pocket.

Any other time, I would roll my eyes and go deal with him. But today, with the girl I've dreamed of for years curled up next to me, an unnatural feeling creeps up.

I can't believe he's dragging me away from my one chance with Delilah.

I can't even tell her where I'm going. She doesn't know about my dad. Doesn't know about his habits.

Her brothers do. They found out when we were teenagers. Snuck out to the bar one night and found him floundering in the vapors, while I was leaning over a pool table.

The expressions on their faces were filled with confusion. I had never talked much about my dad, and I think they just thought he was lazy.

I explained our situation to them and they all understood. Henley was a little hurt. He said I should have trusted him enough to tell him. I told him that he'd do the same for his dad. He disagreed but dropped the subject.

None of us ever told Del. I begged her brothers not to. If I'm being honest, I was embarrassed. I didn't want her to pity me or try to fix the situation. I just wanted her to look at me the way she always did.

But, because I kept her in the dark, I had to leave her sitting in the cool morning grass while I ran with my tail between my legs.

She was calling after me, begging me to tell her what was happening, and I just stayed silent. *Dick move, Hudson.*

I couldn't lie to her, and I couldn't tell the truth, so I just walked away. Does that make me pathetic? Absolutely. Do I feel like the world's biggest loser? One hundred percent.

She looked so hurt as I rode away in silence.

I think that was the first time I truly despised my dad. I've done a lot for him over the years, but his actions only affected me. This time, he inadvertently made me hurt Del, which is unacceptable.

I picked him up from outside the bar. Literally. Picked him up off the nasty bar parking lot ground, threw him over my shoulder, and dumped him in my truck.

I drove him home in silence. Can't talk to someone who's blacked out.

I took him to his house and left.

Didn't even get a thank you. Not that I expected one. But this time, after seeing what it cost me with Del, I noticed.

I spent the rest of the day stewing. Remembering the hurt expression Del wore as I rode off.

I want to go back in time to when she was asleep on my chest. I wonder if she'll ever let that happen again? No. Get real, Hudson. I'm sure she was just cold and using my body for warmth.

But, I can't help wonder, maybe she liked it as much as I did? Doesn't matter much now. She'll be so mad at me for the way I left, she won't speak to me for the rest of the week.

That won't work for me.

I need my daily dose of Del.

Maybe I can go over to her house and act like nothing happened?

There's a dinner tonight at the ranch to celebrate our successful roundup. It's a way for Beckett to thank us for helping, but I think it's just an excuse for everyone to get together.

As big as the dark cloud is that hovers over him, he loves having his family around. They are everything to him, even if he doesn't say it.

If I see Del at her brother's house for the first time since the incident, she'll yell at me in front of everyone, and then I'll have to explain what happened. Then everyone will be upset with me.

I've decided to go to her house and offer her a ride to the ranch. A sort of peace offering.

"Hudson, get out of my house!"

I knew deep down she wouldn't just sweep yesterday morning under the rug. I know Del too well to be surprised by this outburst. She's rightfully pissed at me.

"Listen, I'm sorry." Weak and pathetic, but I have to try.

She seems to agree with my assessment. "I don't even want to look at you right now."

That may be true, but it won't deter me. "It was an emergency, Del. You know I wouldn't leave you for any other reason."

She rolls her eyes so hard I'm worried they're going to disappear in her skull. Her tone is eerily calm. "Really, there is no need to lie."

"I'm not lying." I hate that she doesn't believe me.

"Listen... I didn't mean to make you uncomfortable. I didn't even realize what I was doing until I woke up." She sounds nervous... and is that... shame? She's talking about sleeping on me. She thinks that's why I took off so fast? If only she knew how wrong she is.

"No!" It comes out frantic, and her eyes pop open at my volume. "There really was an emergency."

She signals for me to keep going. "At the bar...there was a customer who refused to leave."

Now, this is only half a lie. At the bar across town, my dad did refuse to leave. She thinks I'm talking about the bar I own, the one that's popular in town. Not very often, but occasionally, someone gets unruly, and I have to deal with them.

I don't often talk about it, and not many people know, but I own the Fortunate Fox bar in town. Del and her family know I own it. Her brother even helped me seal the deal.

There was a period in my life when I was heading down the same path as my dad. I was at the bar gambling every night. The difference between him and I was that I put my money in a safe place.

I knew I was good at pool. I had been winning games for my dad since I was eight years old. As a teenager, I learned that I could make my own bets, play, and do whatever I wanted with my winnings.

I had everything I wanted, though. I lived and worked on the ranch. I was content. Henley was already making a substantial income as a high-profile hockey star in the city, and he advised me to make an investment with my money. Something that would ensure my future.

So, I used my money to buy the place that gave it to me. Henley wasn't convinced this was a good plan since he knew how much trouble it brought me in my youth. But I had a plan.

I turned it from a dive bar to an upscale hangout. Now, don't get me wrong, it's still a small-town bar through and through—pool tables in the corner, glowing Hamm's signs, wood-paneled walls. I just made it known that riffraff wouldn't be tolerated. My dad included.

After a few months of my new, anonymous ownership, my dad and his crew of lowlifes set up shop at the bar outside of town.

I think deep down, buying the bar was a way for me to have some control over my life. It was my idea of cleansing myself of my past. Paradoxical, I know.

She nods her head slowly at me, like she can't decide if I'm telling the truth. "The bartender had been working all night and couldn't get the guy to leave." True, just not at my bar. *Leave her and lie to her. Real nice, Hudson.*

She looks down at her hand, her fingers twisting together. "You didn't say anything. You just left me there."

She's making me feel worse than I already do. "Trust me, there is nowhere I want to be more than in your arms." It slips out, but it's too late to take it back.

She lets out a small gasp. My words shocked her. *They surprised me, too.*

Her cheeks are a beautiful pink color. "I have been told I give the best snuggles," she says smugly.

I see what she's trying to do. Pretend like my comment was nothing serious. I can play that game of she wants, but I can't stand the idea of her being wrapped up in anyone else's arms. Her cuddling them.

No.

"I would have to agree." I try to sound calm and nonchalant.

"Yours could use some work, though, big guy." She giggles a little and taps my chest with her palm as she walks past me and into her room.

"Maybe we should do it again, and you can teach me." My tone is suggestive, but she just laughs through her closed bedroom door.

"You'd like it too much! Probably wouldn't be able to control yourself." She's hitting the nail right on the head with that statement. If I would have had just five more minutes with her in that field yesterday morning, I'm not sure I would've been able to keep it together. Her proximity is dangerous to me.

"You might be right about that."

She comes sauntering out of her room in the sexiest dress I've ever seen. Not just on her, but on anyone ever. It's nothing scandalous, just a red gingham sundress. It shows the expanse of her sun-kissed chest and is thin enough to see the outline of her little lace bra. She is so beautiful. And terribly taunting.

No one would mistake her dress for anything other than casual. No one except me. I can't help but notice that it hugs her curves. How that little lace trim at the end caresses her thighs.

She crosses in front of me like she hasn't just stunned me, and bends down to pull her boots on. Her brown, worn leather ones. Nothing frivolous or fancy.

When she bends down, her dress rides up, and I can see the whole expanse of her mouthwatering thighs. I try to look away, but not very hard.

"Keep it in your pants, Hudson. This is a family event." She chastises me.

My face heats from being caught, so I try to play it off. "Come on, I'll drive you."

She huffs a little laugh and starts heading out the door. "Why? So you can abandon me again."

Okay. I see she's not as over it as she's pretending to be. I follow her outside and close the door behind me. "No, because you and I are going out afterwards."

"Is that so?"

"Yes. As an apology for my less-than-chivalrous behavior." That garnishes a laugh.

She tilts her head to the side, like she's trying to decide whether she can stomach any more time around me.

"Fine. Let's go." She spins on her heels and walks right over to my truck.

It feels like a win.

I make my way over to the truck and pull myself into the driver's seat. When I peek over at her, I see that she's trying to hide her smile.

I turn my truck on and listen to the ignition roar before I shift into drive and pull onto the road.

We drive in comfortable silence for a few minutes. The windows are rolled down, so we get a late-afternoon breeze. One of her arms is draped out of the window, and she's waving her fingers in the air.

"I'm fine, by the way." She says this without looking at me, just watching the fields as we drive.

"I didn't think it'd be that easy to bruise an ego as big as yours," I tease.

She looks over at me and rolls her eyes. "I meant my ankle." She must see the realization register on my face because she adds, "Wow, you forgot. Asshole."

She's right. I forgot. And I am an asshole.

"Del, I'm so sorry. With everything-" she cuts me off by holding her hand up dismissively.

"It's fine. You'll just have to make it up to me after dinner." She delivers this statement with a wink. The innuendo sends my blood heading south.

I shift and try not to let my brain go to the gutter.

I know she doesn't mean it the way I'm interpreting it, but my cock doesn't. He wants to apologize by worshipping her.

I need to control myself. I cannot walk into her brother's house with her and a boner in tow.

"What were you thinking?" My voice sounds thick.

She thinks for a minute, even though I know she already has a plan. She likes to torture me with suspense. "You pay for all my drinks?" She says it like a question, but it's a demand.

"I was going to anyway."

"Good boy," she coos and my cock throbs. What a weakling.

"Are you really okay? I mean your ankle."

She shifts and rests her hand over my arm that's resting across the center console. It's not unusual for her to initiate some sort of contact, but it never stops me from feeling butterflies. "I'm all better. Really."

"I'm sorry I left you."

She gives my arm a squeeze. "It's okay, just don't let it happen again.

"Never," I assure her. And I mean it.

She doesn't live far from her brother's ranch. A couple of miles by road. The woods connect the properties, so she can ride her horse over if she wants.

I'm focused on the warm summer sun hitting my face through the windshield and Delilah's soft hand rubbing gently up and down my arm. She may not even be conscious that she's doing it, the movement being so slight.

She moves to her knees and reaches her hand up to my rearview mirror and takes the leather cord in her hands. "Is this what I think it is?"

Suddenly, the gentle warmth of the sun is stifling. I can feel the embarrassment engulf my face.

"Yep."

She unhooks it from the mirror and brings it close to her face for inspection. "I can't believe you kept it all this time." Her breath is wispy, like the discovery is making her emotional.

In her hand is the four-leaf clover she gave me the morning of my driver's license test. When we were kids, she was obsessed with finding one. She said she needed to be able to carry her luck around. As we grew into teenagers, I thought she had abandoned the task of finding one, but I was wrong.

She presented me with the coveted clover and told me to take it. That I needed the luck for my test.

Her giving me that clover was equivalent to a child receiving a unicorn. I could not believe it. Something she spent *years* searching for, and she gave it to me in a heartbeat.

Later, after I successfully passed my test, I pressed it into resin to preserve it and made a leather braid to hold it in place. I've had it on my key chain or hanging in my truck ever since.

It's a reminder of her. A way to keep her close.

"It's the most important thing I own."

She scoffs. "That's a bit dramatic, don't you think?"

Without hesitation, I answer. "To me, it's an extension of you. So, yes, it is the most important thing I own."

What's wrong with me? Why am I spewing my most intimate thoughts to her?

I've been fine for this long without telling her my feelings. Am I spewing because waking up with her on top of me was an insight into what my life could be like? Maybe it's my subconscious begging me to finally take a chance.

She doesn't say anything about my out-of-pocket declaration. Just hums softly and looks out the window for the rest of the drive.

I'm left wondering if I've just made the biggest mistake of my life. Did my declaration freak her out?

Idiot.

Chapter Nine

Delilah

Did I just have a stroke? Did Hudson really just say that? No. He wouldn't have. Which is why I'm now staring out the truck window, contemplating my sanity.

Despite how much I've tried to project my attraction over the years, it has never been transferred.

I've loved him from afar for as long as I can remember. Now, having him say these things is sending me for a loop.

I'd automatically assume he's teasing me, but there is physical proof in between my fingers.

That four-leaf clover I gave him when I was fourteen and he was sixteen is protected and nestled into a beautiful ornament. I can't stop stealing glances at it and running the leather between my fingers.

I let the silence stretch between us for the rest of the drive. He doesn't say anything, so neither do I.

There are a few possibilities: One, he was just joking. As painful as it is, it's also probable. I'm just his friend's weird sister. Two, he let a hidden feeling slip out and is now regretting saying it with the force of a thousand suns. Three, he admitted to having feelings and is waiting to hear my response.

Since I'm not sure which it is, I just pretend he didn't say it and let the silence ride.

I want nothing more than what he said to be true, but I can't let myself get too hopeful.

When we pull up to the house, I see Emmett outside on the lawn in front of the grill. The smoke wafts into the open truck windows, making my mouth water.

I hop out of the truck and am greeted by Cashton's slobbering Basset Hound. "Hi, Connie." I give her a few scratches under her big, floppy ears, and she nuzzles her head on my legs.

When Hudson walks around the truck, Connie lets a deep howl pierce the air, and I can't help but laugh. He looks offended.

I make my way over to the grill. As I approach, Emmett looks past me, presumably at Hudson, and cocks his head in question.

"I was driving by anyway. Figured I'd give the monster a ride." Sentimental Hudson is gone. I look over my shoulder at him, and whatever expression I'm wearing causes his face to fall.

There's a picnic table set up with a plastic tablecloth and a stack of paper plates. I plop down on the seat facing the field.

Hudson and Emmett are talking by the grill. I rip open the package of red plastic cups and pour myself a glass of lemonade from the pitcher.

Cashton and Beckett come out of the house and go straight to the table. Beckett sets down a big bowl of pasta salad, I'm hoping came from the supermarket, because lord knows he can't cook to save his life. Cash is, of course, carrying a package of beers.

I get a hair ruffle and shoulder squeeze from the two before they head off to the grill.

Connie flops down at my feet under the table, entertaining herself by chewing on a bone.

I'm used to being included and being excluded at the same time from them, so it doesn't bother me anymore. I just sit back, enjoy my drink, and watch the horses grazing in the field.

I'll have to bring Izarra over so she can spend some time with her buddies. I know she gets lonely at the house all alone.

The bench creaks next to me as Hudson sits down. I want to shove his massive shoulders away from me, but refrain.

He sets his big hand on my exposed thighs and squeezes, leaving it there as he says, "You look so lonely over here."

Goosebumps erupt across my skin from his warm palm on me. I look at him. Really look at him. His deep brown eyes search mine. "I'm not lonely, this is how these things always go."

He starts rubbing his fingertips on my thigh. All the way up to the hem of my dress and back down. I feel the muscles deep inside me tighten. "What are you doing?" I ask under my breath. We touch in the way friends do, but never as intimately as he's doing now.

He leans in close, his breath dusting across my cheek. "What I've been dying to do for years."

I can feel my mouth hanging open. He chuckles at me but backs away from my face.

I search his eyes, looking for that twinkle I've come to learn means he's taunting me. But I don't see it.

"If this is some kind of joke, I swear-"

"What's the big secret?" Cash plops down across from us, causing Connie to abandon me in favor of her dad.

I jump, so wrapped up in Hudson's essence that I didn't notice him approaching. Hudson looks startled, too, but makes no move to shift away from me.

"I'm just fucking with you, Del!" He says and smacks a hand on my arm. "You look like I walked in on you doing the nasty."

I can't even think of a witty comeback. I feel like he really did walk into something he shouldn't have.

Hudson keeps making these weird declarations and never explaining himself. I feel stuck in an odd limbo.

I feel Hudson's hand tighten on my thigh. The pressure jogs me back to the present. "Ever the diplomat, Cash," I say and tip my drink in his direction.

Beckett and Emmett join us at the table, setting a plate of sizzling burgers in front of us. Hands reach across the table as we all dish up and dig in.

For the most part, we eat in silence. All savoring the food and drinks. Once we've all finished, the guys pass around beers, and conversation picks up again.

"You guys took forever getting those steers back," Beckett mentions.

"Yeah, what were you doing? Having a sleepover?" All my brothers laugh.

Usually, Hudson and I have no problem with finding stray steers, so they know something went awry for us to be gone all night.

"Del twisted her ankle. We stopped to rest for a while." This comes from Hudson.

"Awe, how sweet is that?" Emmett chides us.

It's not uncommon for my brothers to tease us. Hudson's always been nicer to me than they are, so they give him a hard time. Plus, they all knew about my childhood crush and don't let me forget it. What they don't know is that the crush never went away. If anything, it's bloomed into something more.

"It was sweet," I say. "None of you lot would have been so nice to me."

That meets laughter and Cashton saying, "That's probably true. Hudson's always had a soft spot for you. Treats you like a baby."

"He does not!"

"He does and he always has." This comes from my mostly silent oldest brother. Beckett is big and brooding. Not unlike Eeyore.

"You guys are crazy," is how I answer. But, it's true, Hudson has always gone easier on me than my brothers. He was always on my side.

"No, they're right," says Hudson. "I have always had a soft spot for you." His eyes are so genuine. I can't stop the blush that consumes my cheeks.

Yacking noises and barfing gestures are made from around the table.

I just roll my eyes and avoid Hudson's prying ones.

He's still staring at me like I'm the only one at the table. I feel like I'm doing something wrong, and I'm about to get in trouble.

My brothers have shifted the conversation, but Hudson hasn't joined. He's looking at me like I hold all the answers.

Without breaking eye contact, he brings his free hand to my face and lightly cups my jaw. I'm left slack-jawed by the gesture. Then he dusts his fingers across my cheekbone. "You have a ladybug on your face," he whispers almost reverently. He holds the polka-dotted creature in front of my face before it flies away.

"What are you doing?" I whisper-shout at him.

He turns back to the guys but keeps his hand on my thigh, his thumb dragging delicate strokes across my fragile skin.

"We're going out tonight." That stops all conversation and heads immediately spin in our direction.

Hudson, what are you doing?

"The two of you? Are going out together?" Three sets of brown eyes bore into me. My brothers and I all look alike except for our eyes. The boys all have brown, and I have blue.

I don't like what's happening here. They all look angry. Nothing is going on between Hudson and I. No matter how much I wish it to.

I need to say something before they kill him. "We're going to the bar!" It comes out in an unnaturally high pitch. Beckett quirks a questioning eyebrow at me, and I realize I may have just made the situation worse by confirming that yes, we are going out.

They don't understand that it's not in a romantic way. "Do you guys want to come?" I realize that was also the wrong thing to say because Hudson pulls his hand away from me.

I'm left chilled without his presence. His warm, comforting touch feels miles away.

I look to him, but he won't meet my eye. "Yeah, you guys should come." Hearing it sounds like a punch to the chest.

"Wouldn't want to crash a date, you two." Cashton teases. He knows we weren't going on a date, just likes to make everyone uncomfortable.

"It's not a date, I know the rules," Hudson says with humor in his voice, but I can see the way his jaw tenses. I think he's disappointed.

Was it meant to be a date?

No. He would never.

It's me and Hudson.

Best friend's sister. Brothers' best friend.

It would simply never work.

Maybe the fall messed with my head, because I must be hallucinating Hudson's behavior. One minute, he's acting the way I've always dreamed he would. Then, the next, he's acting like his normal self.

It's making me dizzy.

"And it'll benefit you to remember them," Beckett says with no humor in his voice. It's so stern it almost sounds like a threat.

Hudson throws his hands up. "Easy, man."

Suddenly, the air feels tense. Leave it to Cash to break it. "Well, I'll never say no to a date with Hudson! That's not against the rules, is it, Beck?"

He can't keep the smirk off his face, but Beckett doesn't break. "No, I don't care what you two do."

He's so serious. I swear he's as stiff as a statue.

Cash squeals like a schoolgirl and reaches across the table to grab Hudson's hand.

"You're so strange," Hudson says while simultaneously evading Cash's touch.

The guys finish their beers, and I finish my lemonade. We watch the sky turn from blue to orange sherbet—beautiful streaks of yellow and orange slash across the sky.

I stand up and start grabbing used plates to carry to the garbage out back, while the guys are grabbing the leftover food and bringing it inside.

I let the cool breeze of the early evening air capture my loose hair. I love this time of day. When the Earth shifts from warm and bright to cool and dark. The in between period where the light is dim and the heat is broken by dashes of chills.

I'm staring out at the horizon when Beckett walks up next to me. He places a brotherly hand around my shoulder. "I'll drive you to the bar."

I'm initially surprised. Beck is as close to being classified as a hermit as one can be. He spends nearly all of his time at the ranch. Always working.

"You're coming out with us?"

He shakes his head, and I'm even more confused. "You're not coming out? Why would you drive me if you're not going to stay out?"

"You have to get there somehow."

He's right, but he's making it much more complicated than it has to be. "Yes, but Hudson can drive me."

"How will you get home?"

"I can ride with Em and Cash." He's being so weird.

"You know as well as I do that they won't be coming home tonight." I guess he's right about that.

"Then Hudson can take me home."

His jaw tenses. "And you're sure he will be available when you want to leave?" I understand what he's saying. He thinks Hudson will be as available as Emmett and Cash. I can read between the lines. He thinks I'm going to be stranded because the guys will all go home with someone.

The idea of Hudson going home with some random girl makes my stomach twist. I'm not naive enough to think he doesn't get around. We're all adults and can find pleasure wherever we choose.

I still don't like to think about it, though.

"He'll be available if I ask him."

Deep down, he knows it's true. He knows Hudson would never do something that would put me in harm's way. "I don't mind," he reassures.

I smile at him. He may be a day away from officially becoming a grumpy old man at the age of thirty something, but he's still a softy who cares about his baby sister. "Thank you, but I'll be okay."

The rest of the guys come battling out of the house. My brothers race to their respective trucks and make to pull out of the driveway.

Hudson walks up to Beck and I. "Ready to go?"

I nod and start making my way to the truck. He opens the door for me, and I hop into the cab. I notice Beckett shooting daggers in our direction. What's his deal? I'm an adult just like him. I've been taking care of myself for a while now.

We chase the sunset all the way downtown and park in front of Hudson's bar, *The Fortunate Fox.*

Part of me hopes my brothers stick around to act as a buffer between me and Hudson. He's been prickly towards me since dinner. But, the wishful part of me hopes they leave quickly so I can have a few minutes alone with him.

Chapter Ten

Delilah

My brothers are disgusting and don't last more than an hour before they're walking out of the bar with a woman on each of their arms. If I did that, it would be the end of days. But, no. Apparently, everyone is accustomed to them being dogs, so no one says a thing.

I just roll my eyes and sip my pina colada. I watched Hudson just about crumble from mortification when I asked for one, but he made it without complaint and even put a tiny umbrella in my glass.

Around here, it's beer, bourbon or brandy. Some of the fancy ladies like wine, but *mixed drinks* are simply not on the menu. If your seventy-year-old grandpa wouldn't drink it, they don't serve it here.

As much as it pains Hudson, I love a fruity drink. I'm convinced the only reason he has the ingredients for the drinks is because he knows it's all I like.

No one else in town drinks them, so he does not need to keep everything in stock. Yet, it's always here on the off chance I want one.

One time I ordered an appletini. He visibly cringed but got to work. I watched him make it. Shaking the liquids together in that silly metal drink mixer. His arms looked so sexy. A black, short-sleeved shirt showcased his muscles and intricate tattoos. Then he reached under the counter and pulled out a martini glass.

Mind you, this bar does not serve martinis.

Yet, there was one. A glass specific to a drink that only *I* drink in town.

Do I get funny looks for holding a drink with an umbrella in it? Sure. Do I care? No. I'd much rather drink something that tastes good.

The bar is busy tonight, and a crowd of out-of-towners is lining the bar and crowding the pool tables. Hudson stepped behind the bar to help a bartender make drinks for a large group.

Left to my own devices, I wander from the bar and head over to the pool tables.

At the far end of the bar, four tables are set up in a square formation. Each table has a stained glass light hanging over it, creating a warm glow. There's a group of guys playing around them, so I join the crowd, leaning against the wood-paneled walls.

I can tell these guys aren't from around here simply by looking at their shoes. The uniform shoe in town is cowboy boots. It's just impractical to wear anything else. The dirt, dust, and animal droppings see to that.

These guys are clad in loafers. Classic city shoe. They may look nice, but they aren't functional.

These guys must be taking a weekend trip away from the city. In a town this small, we need the tourists to widen the dating pool. Or, more appropriately, the one-night stand pool.

I've gone home with my fair share of city boys. Nothing to write home about, but they get the job done.

If everyone is going home with someone tonight, I will be too. I've watched Hudson with women before. It feels like a tent stake shooting through my chest, but I've gotten used to it.

I know once he gets out from behind the bar, he'll find a woman and head out.

I'd prefer to be occupied when that happens.

"Hey, darling." I spin around and find a handsome man looking down at me. He's tall. Not as tall as Hudson. Ugh. Is it possible to not compare every man to him?

He's got nice eyes and a sharp jaw. I flash him a sweet smile as I spin to face him. "Hi, there."

His eyes drag down my body and back up slowly before he meets my eyes again. His tongue drags across his lips as he examines me. "You look beautiful in that dress."

My cheeks grow warm. "Thank you," I say sweetly. I'm wearing a simple sundress, but the red and white gingham pattern brings out the color of my eyes. At least that's what Hudson always says.

Did I wear this dress because I know he likes it? I don't want to answer that.

I like it.

It's just a bonus that he does too.

I need to stop thinking about Hudson while the guy in front of me is looking at me like he wants to take my clothes off.

"My boys and I are playing some pool. Want to play a few rounds with us? I can help you if you don't know how to play."

I don't know how to play, but I also don't have any burning desire to learn. But, I fix a smile on my face and say I do.

He's cute enough to suffer through a few rounds of pool.

He puts a hand on my lower back and walks me over to the table that his friends have gathered around. They all appear relatively similar, with simple hairstyles and clean-cut features. All handsome, but nothing spectacular.

All the guys check me out when I walk up to them. The man leans into my ear and whispers, "I'm Brody, by the way." Then he pulls back and looks to his friends with a smug look. As if he won a competition I'm not aware of.

The overall atmosphere shifts into an uncomfortable one.

I kind of want to go back to the bar and wait for Hudson to finish, but when I look in that direction, I don't see him.

Dread settles in my chest. Did he leave? Leave me all alone?

I look back towards Brody and try to take a deep breath.

"What's your name, beautiful?" All the guys are staring at me, and I'm starting to feel overwhelmed. I wish I knew where Hudson was. Just knowing he was still here would put me at ease, but I don't see him.

I feel a hand wrap around my shoulders and settle on my sternum. I'm hit with a strong scent of pine and immediately feel at ease, leaning back into Hudson and settling my back to his front.

He keeps his hand there, possessively in the center of my chest.

"Her name is Delilah. But it would benefit you to forget that."

Brody takes a step back and throws his hands in the air. "Easy, man. We're just having some fun. Gonna play some pool if you wanna join."

I come up to Hudson's shoulders, and I feel his chest rising and falling against my back. I tip my head up to look at him. His dark brown eyes soften when he looks down at me.

He keeps his hand resting on my sternum. "Do you want to play?" He asks gently.

What I really want to do is stay frozen in this moment forever. His hands on me. Him looking at me like I hold the answers of the universe.

"Brody was going to teach me how to play," I say to him.

The muscles in his jaw tense, and he secures me even closer to his body. Not even a millimeter of space is between us. I can feel every hard line of muscles pressed into my soft skin.

He swipes a loose piece of hair behind my ear and leans down to whisper in it. His warm breath tickles my cheek as he whispers, "If you want to learn, I'll be the one teaching you. If I see his hands on you one more time, he and his whole crew will get kicked out. Understand?"

I swallow thickly. He's acting possessive, and I can't help but revel in it. "Yes, I understand," I answer, nodding my head slowly.

He flashes me a sexy grin. "Good girl."

My insides flutter to life, and a warmth spreads throughout my body.

He smiles at me like he knows what those words do to me. His fingertips drag from my collarbone down to my stomach, where he decides to leave his hand.

"We'll play," Hudson declares, and Brody and his friends nod. They look nervous. Probably because Hudson is taller than them and packed with muscle they can only dream of possessing.

"Okay. You and I can take this table. Your girl can have the next one with Justin." He inclines his head towards the table next to us, where a guy wearing a Hawaiian shirt stands with a grin.

I put my hand over the one Hudson has against my stomach. My silent request for him not to leave me.

He must understand because he says, "No." Our fingers twist together. "She stays with me."

Brody gives a humorous laugh. "Maybe you don't know how pool works, but it's a two-person game."

"I'm familiar." He waits a moment before he continues. "My girl says she wants to learn how to play, so I'll be teaching her."

He just called me his girl. What is happening? It sounded so right. So comforting. Against my better judgment, I brush my fingers over his knuckles. I swear I hear a sharp inhale from him when my fingers dust over his.

"Fine," Brody says gruffly.

He sets up the pool balls in their specific pattern and gets his stick ready. Hudson steps away from me to get a stick for me.

Goose bumps appear on my arms when he backs away, and I wrap my arms around myself in an attempt to fight off the newfound chill.

"Here," he said, and places a stick in my hand.

He's acting like this is totally normal. Well, it's not! "Hudson, what are you doing?"

"I'm teaching you how to play pool."

I roll my eyes at his obtuseness. "No, I mean you going all macho and calling me your girl."

He stops rubbing the blue powder on the tip of the stick and locks his eyes with mine. "Was I not being clear earlier?"

I look into his eyes, searching for any sort of hint as to what's going on. All I see is a deep yearning. "Hudson, please just tell me what's going on," I plead.

He sets the chalk down on the table and hands the stick to me. I wrap my fingers around it and wait for his answer.

His hand runs down his face and rubs his jaw while he stares at me.

"If this is some weird way of looking after me at my brothers' orders, you can drop it."

"It's not."

That's all he's going to say? I feel like he's being evasive on purpose. "Then what's happening here?" I feel vulnerable asking.

"I'm teaching you how to play pool." Then he places a hand on my back and leads me to the pool table.

I guess that's the end of the conversation.

"Ready?" Brody asks. Hudson nods, and he leans down on the table with his stick lined up to take his first shot. He pulls the stick back and propels it forward, hitting the cue. The moon-looking ball shoots towards the triangle of balls and clicks on impact. The colored balls shoot in all directions around the table. A few go into the pockets, but it happens so fast that I'm not sure which ones.

Brody moves around the table a few times, hitting more balls in before a red ball misses the pocket and ricochets back into the center of the table. He steps back and looks our way smugly.

Did he do a good job? I honestly have no idea.

I look to Hudson for what to do next, and he walks to the table with me. "You're going to try to hit the balls with the stripes on them."

He walks me to the back left corner of the table and points at a ball with orange stripes across from us. "Put that one," he points to the ball, "in that pocket," he points to the nearest pocket.

"Oh, and make sure to hit the cue first."

I roll my eyes at that, and he chuckles in response.

I lean down across the table and position my stick in front of the cue. I feel Hudson position himself behind me. His body pressed against the back of my legs.

I look over my shoulder at him. "What are you doing?"

I can feel his muscles tense as he looks down at me, bent over in front of him. "Your dress is very short, Del."

Instantly, I flush. It's hard to focus with him towering over me like this. His waist lined up perfectly with my ass. If I pushed back I'd be able to feel his cock.

I fling my stick forward, nicking the cue, but not moving it anywhere.

I make to stand up since I just blew my turn, but Hudson keeps my body in place.

He reaches around me and moves the cue ball back to where it was before I shot at it.

"Hey man! What are you doing?" Hudson looks over towards Brody and glares.

"She's trying again," he declares.

That causes Brody to let out a huff. "That's not how the game works, dude."

Hudson's smile looks dangerous. "It is tonight. My bar, my rules." The declaration causes Brody to fluster and stay quiet.

He puts a hand in the center of my back and pushes slightly until I'm once again leaning over the table. The gesture feels oddly sexual, and our current position is no different.

He bends down and leans over my body, wrapping his arms around mine, and puts his hands over mine that are on the pool stick.

I can feel his warm breath on my neck. The veins of his arms brushing mine. The stubble on his cheek. His steel cock pressing into my ass.

I shift slightly to try to feel more. He growls in my ear and whispers, "What are you doing, ladybug?"

I wiggle again and feel his length rub against the seam of my ass. I hold in the gasp I so desperately want to release.

"You're distracting me," I whisper back.

"*I'm* distracting *you*?" He asks incredulously.

"Yes, I can feel you..."

"So, have you finally realized what you do to me?"

My throat feels thick as I swallow. I try to focus back on the game, but his soft breath against my sensitive flesh makes it impossible.

I want to push back and feel him again. To double-check it's as huge as it felt before.

He helps me pull back the stick and fire it directly into the cue ball, which in turn hits the orange-striped ball, sending it smoothly into the pocket.

He did all the work, but he made me feel like I did it all on my own.

We take a few more shots like that until I get the hang of it by myself.

I'm not nearly as skilled without Hudson guiding me, but I go on to play a few more games under Hudson's watchful eye. I lose every time, but he praises me like I'm doing better than the other guys.

I put my stick back in the wooden rack and walk over to Hudson. As soon as I'm in reach, he wraps his arm around my waist and pulls me in close.

Butterflies fly freely around my stomach and chest. He's been so touchy with me tonight, and I can't help but thrive under it.

I lean against him and let out a deep yawn. It has to be getting late. We arrived when the sun was fading and have been playing games for hours.

"Ready to call it a night, ladybug?" His tone is so tender. I melt even deeper into his hold and nod my head.

"Okay, let me get you home."

We turn and start to walk away, but are interrupted by an obviously intoxicated Brody.

"Hey! Where are you going, sweet thing?" His question is posed towards me.

"Umm..." I look to Hudson and see fire burning behind his eyes. "I'm going home."

Brody lets out a snicker. "Why don't you sit down, let me finish this game, and then you can come home with me?"

Hudson's whole body tenses. The hand on my hips tightening to a painful pressure, and his other hand balls into a fist.

Eager to remedy this situation, I say, "No. I'm going home with him."

Hudson looks at me, and for that moment, his eyes soften, adoration evident in his gaze. Then idiot Brody has to ruin it. "How about this," he starts like there is any chance I would go with him. "Me and your friend play, and whoever wins gets to take you home."

I fight back the urge to gag and laugh in his face simultaneously.

Is this seriously his best attempt to get my favor? If he can't tell that he stands no chance against the man who currently has his arms wrapped around me in a death grip, then he is the biggest fool I've ever encountered.

No woman wants to be the prize one wins after a lousy game of pool in a small town bar.

Hudson's breathing is shallow. I look up at him, waiting for him to say something and take me out of here, but he's already staring at me. His eyes are pleading, and he looks terrified.

Does he honestly think I would want that? That I would choose to spend even a second with that mouth breather when I could have him?

His arms are bound around me tightly, but I wiggle and turn in them until my chest is pressed against his. I push up onto my tip toes, bringing our faces level.

Staring into his eyes, having his protective arms around me, I get a burst of confidence. I bring my hands to his face and hold his cheeks in my hands. Then I lean even closer, until our breath is mixing.

I can feel his heart beating erratically against my chest. His gaze darts to my lips and licks his own like he's dreaming of tasting me.

I close the unbearable distance between us, and I seal my lips over his.

He doesn't waste a second and kisses me back.

His lips are so soft against my own, but the stubble on his face is rough, causing the most incredible mix of sensations.

Fire dances down my spine as I feel his tongue against the seam of my lips. He coaxes them open and slips his tongue into my mouth.

He tastes of the spices in his drink, and I'm desperate for more.

We keep on kissing, forgetting about the world around us. All that matters now is Hudson. His lips on mine, his hands trailing up and down my back.

We kiss like we're afraid of stopping. Our tongues are gentle, but our lips are determined.

He starts to withdraw, teasing me by dragging my bottom lip out with his teeth. I whimper at the loss of him and pout my bottom lip out.

He looks down at me with reverence, and I can feel the doe-eyed look on my face that matches his.

I chance a glance at his lips and find them swollen and damp from our kiss.

I'm desperate for more.

He must be feeling the same burning I am because he bends down and scoops me up in his arms, holding me bridal style against his chest.

Curled up next to him, I can feel the heat he's radiating. I tuck my head against the crook of his neck and place a delicate kiss just below his jaw.

He lets out a deep groan that makes the spot between my thighs throb.

Pushing his way through the crowded bar, he walks straight to the stairwell leading to his apartment upstairs.

He marches up the stairs like I weigh nothing, pushing open his front door, walking us over the threshold, and using his foot to slam the door behind us.

He sets me down on the ground in front of him, keeping me steady with his hands on my waist, and says, "I've been dreaming about this moment for as long as I can remember."

Chapter Eleven

Hudson

Her doe eyes gaze up at me with a longing I've never seen before. Her tits heave under the confins of her dress I so desperately want to strip off her.

She's standing in front of me, pleading with her eyes for me to make a move.

I brush her hair away from her neck and let my fingertips brush her exposed collarbone.

Her skin is so soft under my rough fingers. It almost feels wrong to have someone as rugged as me marring her immaculateness.

Almost.

I'm not strong enough to stop the pull between us in this moment. Every reason I have to stop disappears. I don't care if her brothers find out. I need her more than I need my next breath.

My fingers find the loose straps of her sundress on the tops of her shoulders. I tease her skin with gentle brushstrokes before I finger the knots.

She sucks in sharp breaths and looks at me. Her mouth is parted in the sexiest way.

"Do you want me?" I chance the question. I need to know before the last bit of my restraint slips.

She rests her hands on my chest and drags her nails down my muscles. My body shivers in response.

"Do *you* want *me*?" Her voice is so timid. I can't hold in the laugh that bursts from my lips.

She pales, and I see hurt flash in her eyes.

"I want you in ways that would terrify you," I'm quick to remedy.

She stares at me with wonder, and my muscles tremble from the power I'm using to keep myself under control.

"Now tell me," I demand. "Do you want me?" I feel so vulnerable in the moments I wait for her response.

She could laugh in my face. Run to her brothers and tell them everything. Then I wouldn't just lose her, but I'd lose all of them.

"Yes." She bows her head ever so slightly, like she's embarrassed. Her eyes are cast down to the floor. I don't like that.

I grab her chin in my fingers and force her to look at me. She is flushed red, and her eyes are glassy.

I need to bring her out of this shell she's suddenly decided to grow. "Tell me how you want me." I may be pushing her right now, but I need to hear her tell me what she wants.

The blush on her cheeks travels down to her neck and grows impossibly darker.

"I... I um..." She stutters over her words and tries to fight my grip and look away from me.

I take her small hand and bring it up to my chest, resting it directly over my pounding heart. "I'm nervous too," I whisper.

Exposing my vulnerability is new to me, but I want to make her comfortable. I want her to know that I'm feeling the same way she is.

"I want you to touch me." I'm so proud of her for using her voice.

I flash her a genuine smile. "So do I, ladybug."

She smiles back at me, but I don't make any move to touch her anywhere besides the residual touch she must feel from my fingers running along her dress straps.

"May I?" I want to see every inch of her. Feel her skin press against my own.

She nods vehemently, and I can't help but chuckle at her eagerness.

Without wasting a second, I pull the strings loose and let them fall. Her dress follows, and it slips down her body until it's pooled on the floor around her ankles.

I just stare at her for a moment. I've seen her in this little clothing before, but she was in a swimsuit and we were at the lake with her family. Now she's standing in front of me in a lacy little bra and matching panties. She looks ethereal as the moonlight shines through the windows and onto her skin.

She tries to cover her stomach with her arms, but I grab her wrists and pull them away. I don't want her to hide from me. "No. I want to see you."

She squirms in my hold like she's not sure what to do with herself.

I want to put her at ease. "You are beautiful, Delilah." Her breathing picks up at my words, and I cup her face with my hands, rubbing soothing circles on her jaw.

Her eyes drop from mine down to my lips. I smirk at her before leaning down and kissing her. I start slow, teasing her. Kissing her gently and moving my lips down to her jaw.

My lips are soft as I trace the angles of her face down to her neck, but I increase my pressure and leave open-mouthed kisses.

She lets out a delicious whimper when I nip at her collarbone, and I can't help but groan in response.

Her body is pressed against mine, and I feel her hips canting, searching for friction.

My girl wants me bad.

She's not alone in that feeling.

Without warning, I pick her up by the back of her thighs, and she lets out a surprised yelp. She instinctively wraps her arms around my neck and her legs around my waist. Our chests are pressed together, and her warmth seeps into me.

In this position she can grind on my cock with more success. I feel her hot center through our layers of clothes, and she adjusts to the perfect angle and throws her head back on a moan.

I squeeze her ass in my hands and walk her through the apartment to my bedroom.

Dropping her on my bed, I crawl over her. She spreads her thighs for me, inviting me in.

She starts frantically pushing my shirt up, pleading with me to take it off. I oblige her and throw it onto the floor next to my bed.

She runs her hands over my chest and down to my stomach. I can feel the heat running through me as she traces each groove of muscle.

My cock is throbbing painfully. The sight of her lying under me in nothing but her bra and panties is mesmerizing.

She looks like she belongs there.

I kiss her frantically, not letting either of us catch our breath.

Her nipples harden against my chest and pull the fabric hiding her breasts away.

I pinch the bud between my thumb and forefinger, and she breaks our kiss to cry out in pleasure.

I take the opportunity to kiss my way down her sternum and take her nipple into my mouth.

To start, I kiss around it, letting it grow impossibly firm. Then, I graze it with my teeth, giving her a short zap of pain before I seal my lips around it and suck, allowing her to experience her pleasure.

My finger traces a circle around her other nipple before I tap the bud a few times. Then I roll it between my fingers.

Her satisfied moans circle me like a spell, and I can feel that familiar electricity of my own approaching orgasm in my spine. All I'm doing is touching her, hearing her, seeing her, and it's enough to have me nearly exploding.

I switch my mouth to her other nipple and give it the same treatment. Both of her rosy peaks are swollen and wet when I pull away.

She writhes beneath me as I kiss a trail down her stomach and stop at her panties. I can smell her sweet nectar and find a damp patch in the middle of the fabric. I look up at her from between her legs and flash her a grin.

"Hudson, please. I need you!" Her breath is so airy and desperate that I couldn't possibly deny her.

I trace her wet spot with my finger. "You're soaked for me."

After pressing a kiss over the spot, I use my hands to peel her panties out of my way, throwing them to the floor.

Now, nothing separates us.

She shivers and tries to close her legs. I palm her inner thighs and push them as far apart as she can comfortably handle. "Thats my pussy and I want to see it."

She whimpers at my words but doesn't resist my hold on her.

My girl seems to be rather pliant in bed, the complete opposite of how she acts outside of it.

Her pussy is glistening, so wet that its dripping down the seam of her asshole.

"Please," she cries, and I oblige her, dipping my head to her center and pressing and feather light kiss on her clit.

"Like that, ladybug?" I know it's not enough, but I want to hear her say it.

She reaches for my head and tries to push my face towards her pussy. "No, more!"

My sweet girl sounds so desperate for me. I kiss her again, but this time I stay, licking from her opening to her clit. The taste of her cum erupts on my tongue. She is so sweet, and wet, and warm.

I suction my lips around her nub and suck. She moans in ecstasy as she digs her nails into my scalp.

Her cries don't deter me, I know she's feeling nothing but pleasure, so I lick and suck her as she chants my name. My chest swells with pride that I'm the one doing this to her, seeing her like this.

She wants *me*.

I take a finger and massage her opening before I slide it deep inside her.

"Holy shit," she moans. "It's so intense."

I only have one finger in her, and she already feels so tight. I try not to think about how tight she'll squeeze my cock. If I do, I'll certainly lose my composure and come in my pants.

Slowly pumping in and out of her, I drag deep guttural moans from her pretty mouth.

Her eyes are sealed shut as her pleasure becomes too intense. I take this opportunity to lean down and suck on her clit again.

Her tiny legs start to tremble around my palm, and her fingers tighten painfully in my hair.

I want to drag this out, keep her a trembling mess for hours before I finally allow her to come, but I need to see her fall apart for me. Now.

Gently, I graze my teeth over her swollen bud, and she comes undone. Her legs tremble, and her scream pierces the air. I've never seen anything as beautiful as Delilah coming undone for me.

She continues to shake and I soother her with soft kisses around her pussy. "You did so well, beautiful," I praise.

When she finally settles, I pull back and admire her swollen pussy. My mouth waters as the taste of her remains in my mouth.

Her eyes are hooded, but she wears a satisfied smile. "That was incredible," she says sleepily, her eyes falling closed.

My poor girls are about to pass out on me. The orgasm is so intense that it's literally knocking her out.

I crawl up the bed and settle next to her. She curls up against me, resting half her body on top of me.

The girl of my dreams is falling asleep on me because of how intense the orgasm *I* gave her was.

Life can't get better than this.

She nuzzles her face deeper into my chest, and I squeeze my arms around her, pulling her impossibly closer to me.

Sleepily, her hand starts rubbing up and down my stomach until she dips lower and her hand lands on my aching cock.

She lets out a gasp when she feels me, and I try not to swell with caveman pride.

"What about you?" She asks in her quiet, sleepy voice while starting to rub the length of me.

There's nothing I want more on this planet than to allow her to touch me, but my girl is minutes away from falling asleep. She needs her rest.

I place my hand over hers and move it back to my stomach. "Not tonight, my sweet girl. Now you sleep."

She angles her face towards mine so our eyes meet. "But you didn't get to finish..." she trails off.

"Trust me, tasting your pussy was the most pleasurable thing I've ever experienced."

I lean down and press a long kiss to her forehead, ignoring my cock which is so hard I fear it may burst, and instead focus on her breathing.

After a few minutes of rubbing soothing circles on her back, her heart rate starts to slow, and her breathing evens out.

I watch her sleep tucked into my side until I eventually drift off, closing out the best day of my entire life.

Chapter Twelve

Hudson

W aking up with Delilah spread across me has got to be the same feeling as nirvana.

Her soft brown hair is tickling my face, and the soft smell of pears is invading my senses.

Her little body is wrapped tightly around mine, with her leg, arm, and half of her body thrown over mine. She's holding me as if she's worried I'll slip away.

Someone could cement me in this exact position, and I would thank them for it.

I've been lying here for a few hours just watching her sleep.

I'm usually up before the sun rises to get started on work at the ranch. Del, on the other hand, prefers a more leisurely approach to starting the day.

Today, I don't mind one bit.

I'm going to soak up this moment for as long as it lasts.

Delilah doesn't do anything she doesn't want to do. I'm not afraid that she'll regret last night. I am, however, worried she'll convince herself that it was a one-time thing.

It certainly was not some spur-of-the-moment decision for me, and I don't think it was for her either.

I felt the way she clung to me. The way her voice quivered when she told me she wanted more.

She fell asleep almost immediately last night, meaning she's wearing only her white lace bra, which means her practically naked body is draped across mine. Torture or blessing, I can't decide.

The arm I have wrapped around her is dragging soft lines up and down her hip to her waist.

I only got my shirt off last night, and her cheek is resting directly against my heart; her soft breath hitting my bare skin.

She starts to shift, and I instinctively tighten my grip on her waist. I don't want her to slip away.

She settles for a moment before she drags her hand that's resting on my stomach up to my chest. Her nails dig in as if she's trying to figure out what's underneath her, and I watch the moment she remembers where she is.

Her brows scrunch, and a beautiful red hue decorates her freckled nose.

"Hudson?" Her voice is light and questioning.

"It's me, Del." I use my other hand to brush a loose strand of hair behind her ear and find her staring up at me.

"What are you doing here?" Her voice is raspy and adorable.

"This is my house, Del."

Her blush deepens, and she uses her elbow to prop herself up on my chest. Now, she looks down at me, and her hair falls over our faces like a veil, effectively shutting us out from the world.

Her eyes have always sparkled, but being this close to her, I can see a fleck of brown on the outside of her blue irises that I've never seen before.

"That's not what I meant smart ass."

"I think this is the first time you've ever called me smart," I tease. My hands are still tightly wrapped around her, and I make no effort to move them.

"It's far too early for your quips. I meant, why are you here and not at work?"

I let out a humorless laugh. "I wouldn't have left this bed if it were on fire."

Her smile grows, and I feel my heart picking up speed. "You would have let me burn?"

"It was a metaphor, smart ass." I give her ass a light smack that elicits the most enticing giggle out of her.

Her soft hands frame my face, and she strokes my cheeks with her thumbs, her eyes darting from my eyes down to my lips.

"Can I kiss you?" Her voice sounds meek. Very different from her usual, confident tone.

I drag one of my hands from her back and cup the back of her head. Our faces are so close that our breaths are becoming one. "You never need to ask permission to kiss me."

"Okay." Then she kisses me. Soft and light. An exploration of sorts. She takes her time learning the shape of my lips and lets me do the same to her. Last night I was frantic, but now I can take my time.

I kiss her back, just as softly, my hands exploring her body while her hands stay planted on my jaw. She uses her position to angle my head just the way she wants it.

I let her guide us. She sets the pace and intensity, and gratefully, I accept.

I've spent the better part of my life wondering what Del would feel like in my arms. How soft her skin would feel. How sweet her lips would taste.

Nothing I've ever imagined compares to the real thing.

We stay connected for what feels like hours. Our hands exploring and our mouths learning one another.

Her body shivers, and I feel goosebumps erupt on her arms.

I selfishly forgot that she was nearly naked. I enjoyed the feel of her skin against mine too much.

Now she's cold despite the heat burning between us.

I shift our position so she's beneath me. We're both breathing heavily, and she's begging me with her eyes to keep going.

She wraps her hands around my neck and tries to pull me back to her lips, but I hold strong. As much as I want to kiss her until the end of time, I will not allow her to be cold and uncomfortable.

"No more."

Anger flashes in her eyes. "Why not?"

I dust my knuckles across her cheek. "I need to get you warmed up and then some food in your belly."

"I can think of a few ways you can warm me up." Then the little minx wraps her legs around my waist and pulls me close to her. Her lips tickle my ear as she whispers low and seductively, "Plus, I owe you for last night."

A deep groan rolls out of me. I want nothing more than to strip her bare and spend the next several hours inside of her, but I need her to know she owes me nothing.

"You'll have plenty of chances to make it up to me, but first, breakfast." I kiss the tip of her nose and push away from her despite her protests.

I find my shirt from last night and give it to her to wear. She slides it over her head and lets it cover her.

I hold back the desire to kiss her again. If I start, I won't be able to stop. She just looks so damn perfect wearing *my* clothes, sitting in *my* bed.

I scoop her up bridal style and head to the kitchen. "What does this mean?"

"What do you mean?"

"I mean, do I have to go back to pretending I don't imagine what you look like with your shirt off every time I see you?"

"It'd be pretty difficult since you've seen it up close and personal."

"I'm serious," she swats my chest.

"So am I, but before we discuss that, I need you to elaborate on just how often you imagine me naked." I laugh.

"I do not imagine you naked!" She shrieks.

"Well, now I feel like a creep because I think about you naked all the time."

"You do?"

"Yes, Del.. Probably more than I should."

"But why?"

"Why?"

"Yeah, why?"

"Because you are the most beautiful woman I have ever laid eyes on. Because your smile alone is enough to get me hard. Because I have had a crush on you since I was eight years old and have dreamed of you feeling the same way for equally as long."

I think this is the first time since I've known Del that she's speechless. Her mouth opens and closes, but she doesn't say anything.

She nuzzles her head against my chest, speaking into it and says, "I've had a crush on you since the first day you came to the ranch."

A sense of joy and pain mix in my veins. Joy because she wants me. She feels the same way I do about her. Pain because we missed out on so much time together.

I tighten my grip on her and kiss the top of her head. "No more wasting time apart."

"Is this real, Hudson? It feels too good to be true."

"This is real, baby," I confirm and set her down on the bar stool sitting at my kitchen counter. "Now, what do you want for breakfast?"

Before she can answer, I get started on making us eggs and toast, stopping every few seconds to steal a kiss. She giggles every time, and I feel like the king of the moon.

The eggs sizzle in the pan, and the smell of warm bread permeates the air.

I just set a plate of food in front of Del when my front door flies open and bangs against the wall.

Whoever is interrupting my morning with Del better be ready to die, because that's precisely what's going to happen.

"What the hell!" I shout as I leave the kitchen and head towards the front of the apartment where the noise came from.

I come face-to-face with three of Delilah's brothers. A layer of ice fills my veins, but I try not to let it show on the outside.

I didn't even think about them last night. I was so captivated by my girl that I didn't even think about the consequences.

If they see her here, it's over. They'll kill me and I won't be able to be with her.

But now that my lust-filled haze has lifted, I'm seeing this situation in a fresh light. How can I be with Delilah without losing her brothers? How can I go another day without her, knowing she's wanted me for as long as I've wanted her?

I can't.

I can't lose Del.

But I also can't lose her brothers. They're the best friends I've ever had. I consider them my family.

"Sorry for the door, but we can't find Del anywhere! She's not at her house or the ranch. We know she was at the bar last night, so we need to know who she went home with. We're freaking out here, man."

I forget for a moment that she's sitting safe in the next room, because ice floods my veins. I think it's contagious because I feel it as much as there are.

The idea of her being missing is enough to set all of us into a tailspin. And I saw her ten seconds ago!

"Emmett?" Her soft voice breaks the tension, and then she rounds the corner. Barefoot, wearing my shirt that's big enough to swallow her whole.

I tense and brace myself for the inevitable onslaught of fists that are about to hit me in the face.

But they don't come.

Three bodies that rival the size of my own push past me and embrace Del.

They all do the brother size-up. Ensure everything is in the same condition as when they left it.

I feel a bead of sweat slide down my neck. Can they tell I touched her? Do they know I held her naked body in my arms all night?

"We've been losing our minds, Del." Cash grabs her by the shoulders and pulls her into his arms.

Emmett joins in their group hug, wrapping his arms around both of them, squeezing tightly. Beckett stands near me and watches.

"How long have you been here?" Emmet asks. "Neither of you was answering your phones," he says over his shoulder to me.

My body tenses. I was in a completely different world with Del. I didn't think about anything besides her.

"I crashed here last night since you all ditched me and went god knows where!" She throws her arms up in the air.

"You what?" This comes from Stone Cold Beckett beside me.

"We didn't do anything," and "She's lying" come from both Cashton and Emmett.

"Did you two leave Lilah alone at a bar?" His tone has the ability to silence us all and send a shiver down my spine.

"Hudson was there when we left, so it's his fault."

"My fault?"

"Yeah, you were the last one to see her." Cash sounds like he's trying to blame me for something.

"Yes, and she's fine," I throw a hand in her direction to find her already staring at me.

"Maybe a little too fine if you ask me," Emmett singsongs. "Is that your shirt, my baby sister is wearing?"

A small hand pushes Emmett, sending him toppling into the wall. "Unlike you lot," she throws her hand in the direction of her brothers, "Hudson didn't abandon me last night."

"Still doesn't answer why you're wearing his clothes," Emmett pitches in.

These two idiots are just trying to save their own skin. They both know Beck is going to give them hell for leaving her alone. They're just trying to shift the focus away from themselves.

"Was I meant to leave her to her own devices? Was I to allow her to find her own, more questionable, lodging for the evening? I think you all know she was safer here than she would have been anywhere else."

They don't need to know what really transpired between the two of us. All that matters is that she was safe. In my arms. No one else's.

"Thank you, Hudson." Becket shocks the room. He's a man of few words, and nearly all of them are unpleasant. "We all know there is no safer place for Lilah, besides us, than Hudson."

Pride swells in my chest. I know he doesn't know my true feelings for her, but his words feel like a blessing.

"Let's go, Del. We will drop you off at home." He puts a hand on her back and starts walking her to the door.

"It's okay, Hudson can take me."

"We're driving back to the ranch, we'll drive right past your house. Doesn't make sense to make him drive all the way out there and back." He shifts her body in front of his and ushers her out the door, then signals his brothers out too.

She shoots me a longing look over her shoulder before she passes the threshold.

Before he exits, Beck stops and says to me, "You're the only person I trust with her, don't do something to convince me otherwise." Then he's gone and I'm left with a bad taste in my mouth.

His words sounded like a threat, but I intend to do everything in my power to make sure his words remain true. I want to be the one to keep her safe. Keep her happy and satisfied. I want to be the man her brothers trust around her.

I may be deceiving them now by keeping the depth of my adoration for her to myself.

They may think I'm behaving in her best interest because of our friendship, but one day they will come to realize that I have been in love with her for as long as I've known her. They will come to terms with the fact that I will love her until the end of my days.

Delilah doesn't yet know just how strong my feelings for her are, so I can't expect her brothers to.

But one day she will, and until then, I will continue to be the devoted friend and allow Delilah to set the pace. We didn't get a chance to discuss what this means for us.

I will not allow last night to be the end of our story.

I will give her all the time she needs, but I will not retreat.

We need time to discuss our relationship and the best way to tell her brothers.

Chapter Thirteen

Delilah

Although I have my own business and a means of supporting myself, I am still required to work on the family ranch. It is a requirement that comes with the Walton name.

We all have to *pitch in*, as my brother calls it. He says that my parents would have wanted it this way. All of us working together to ensure the success of the ranch.

I tend to disagree. I think our parents would have wanted us to be happy, regardless of the path we chose.

Emmett and Cash agree with me because they also have careers outside of the family ranch. Emmett is a big rodeo star, and Cash is a farrier.

Beckett's the one who pressures us to stick around.

I don't complain when I get to be out in the fields or working with the animals. That part I love. It's the behind-the-scenes bullshit that drives me up the wall.

I hate paperwork!

It's boring and makes me feel stupid.

Today, Beckett is forcing me to review the financials and confirm orders for this fall.

It's not particularly difficult, I just don't want to do it.

The *office* is the loft above the family barn. It's got an old breakfast table for a desk and a lawn chair for the seat, and there's a window that has an old beach towel acting as a curtain.

All the paperwork is scattered around the room. We don't have a filing cabinet, so we just stack things in piles by year. It's the same system that worked for my parents, so we haven't tried to change it.

Another thing that worked for my parents, which we still use, is the behemoth computer. I wouldn't be surprised if it's older than I am.

It takes a good ten minutes to fire up, and once it's on, you have to save your work every couple of minutes or you risk losing all the work you've already done, because it crashes at random

I mentioned getting a new computer once, but Beckett shot me down. He says it works just fine.

It doesn't, but he wouldn't know that since he never does the paperwork!

I've just finished making my last call for the day and making a digital copy of Mr. Erickson's information.

He wants to start using our beef to feed his ranch hands. He has a large operation on the edge of town and has about a hundred live-in workers. This order will increase our workload but allow the ranch to live more comfortably during the winter months.

Business slows down considerably for us during the winter, so it'll be nice to have his business to help push us through.

I decide to stop at the big house and let Beck know that I'm heading home.

My childhood home hasn't changed much since I've moved out. In fact, Beck has kept it like a shrine to my parents. All the furniture is the same. Every decoration and piece of furniture is in the same place.

It doesn't feel like his house at all.

I push open the giant oak door, but don't stop to take my boots off. I consider the dirt droppings to be payback for interrupting my morning with Hudson the other day.

"Beck! Are you here? I finished up the calls and am heading home," I shout as I walk further into the house. It's late afternoon now, so the guys should be finishing up for the day.

"Del, is that you?" I recognize the deep register of that voice.

I pick up my pace and round the corner into the kitchen. He's standing at the kitchen island wearing faded jeans and a tight grey t-shirt. His boots are just as dirty as mine, and it brings a smile to my face that he's tracking dirt through Beck's house, too.

"Well, hello there," I say as I come to stand next to him. I stop, so only a few inches separate us. This is much closer than we would have stood just a few days ago.

The nearness of our bodies is symbolic of the evolution of our relationship.

This distance is intimate, and the darkness in Hudson's eyes tells me he agrees.

He wraps one arm around my waist and pulls me in even closer, until our bodies are flush. His heat bleeds through the thin layer of my dress, making me feel cozy and happy.

"I missed you," he whispers and drops a kiss to my forehead.

"You saw me a few hours ago." I ran into him when I got here. He looked delicious, loading feed into the truck bed.

I wanted to tell him as much, but he was working with Emmett, so I kept my distance.

We've only had casual encounters since our night together. I would have worried that he regretted it and was trying to pretend it hadn't happened, but when I waved at them as I got out of the vehicle, he very obviously checked me out and then winked at me.

Butterflies erupted in my stomach, and I had to quicken my pace before my brother could see me ogling his best friend.

But now, I have him all to myself. "I was starting to worry you forgot about me," I say, and give him my best pout.

He dips his head in close, his lips brushing my ear, and he whispers, "I have been dreaming about having you in my arms again. I don't think I can go another night without you in my bed."

Where did this Hudson come from?

He's always been kind to me, treated me like a friend. But I never got the impression that he had feelings for me. All my life, I thought I was the pathetic loser crushing on her brother's hot best friend.

Turns out, he's been just as pathetic as I have.

"Well, what's been keeping you away? You know where I live."

He stiffens for a moment before he schools his features. "I had some issues at the bar recently, but don't mistake that for me wanting to be anywhere else than with you."

I'm not sure I believe his excuse. I know he has a full staff at the bar that is fully capable of running the place. As far as I'm concerned, he owns the place on paper alone. He treats the ranch as his job, not the bar.

To this day, I'm not quite sure why he decided to buy it. Or how.

"Well, you'll see me tonight. Right?" Every Sunday, we have a mandatory family dinner. Mandatory makes it sound like a chore. It's more of a regularly scheduled event.

Growing up, every Sunday, my mother would make us all sit around the table together. She would ask us all questions about our week. It was an opportunity for us all to debrief with each other on what was happening in our respective lives.

We spent almost every night together, but she made Sundays a special event. A dinner we didn't usually eat, or follow up the meal with a new movie she rented from the video store.

After we lost our parents, we never stopped our Sunday dinners.

For a while, they helped us through our grief.

Now they fill us with family, laughter, and memory.

"I've never missed a Walton Sunday dinner, and I don't plan on starting now. Especially now that I can sit next to you and feel you up under the table."

The laugh escapes me before I can stop it. "You're so bad."

"Oh, baby, I can be a whole lot worse."

He places a quick kiss on my lips, and it has my insides aching for more. Then, he pulls back and the mother fucker winks at me.

But, before I have a chance to pull him back to me, he walks out the door.

Chapter Fourteen

Delilah

As promised, Hudson walked through the door right on time for dinner.

After working on paperwork this morning, I went home and made a batch of jam before heading back over.

These family dinners are casual, and we come and go as we please. But Beckett always has dinner done by six sharp, and he expects us to be there on time.

He's by no means a chef, but he knows how to grill a steak, which is usually what we have.

He has the patio door open, allowing the smoke from the grill and the cool evening air to blow into the dining area.

I just finished setting out plates and took a seat closest to the door so I could pour myself a glass of sun tea.

Hudson rounds the corner into the dining room and smiles brightly at me.

He looks tired, which makes sense because he's been working in the fields all day and has a red face to prove it. His jeans are stained with dirt, and it looks like he's missing a button on his shirt.

"Tough day?" I ask.

He walks straight towards me with tunnel vision. His eyes are dark and determined as he approaches me.

He stops next to me and drops a kiss to my forehead before sitting in the seat next to me and pulling my chair close to his.

I quickly look around to see if anyone saw him. I haven't mentioned anything to my brothers yet.

After our night together, my brothers were so pissed that I had gone MIA, I assumed that breaking the news of Hudson and I wouldn't go over well.

Then, I didn't see Hudson for a few days, and I was worried he had gotten cold feet, so I didn't say anything.

I know he hasn't said anything to them either because there's no chance in hell my brothers wouldn't have said anything to me if they knew.

"Let's see... I had a good morning. Got to ride out to the south quadrant and found a patch of wild Daliah's. Then came back to grab some lunch and got to see my beautiful girl." I feel my cheeks grow warm. "Then it started to go downhill. Emmett and I were dropping hay, and I got stuck in the bed, throwing the bales. Long story short, he hit a pothole and I went over the side and hit the ground. Hard."

I fight the laugh bubbling in my chest. I can see the movie in my head so vividly. "So, that explains the state of you."

He pouts. "It hurt real bad, love. But I think I know what you can do to make me feel better."

Consider my interest piqued. "Oh, and what would that be?"

"I need you to kiss it better," he winks, and I feel the rest of my blood heat in response.

"Where are you hurt exactly?" I not so subtly look him up and down.

"Everywhere hurts, so I'll need you to kiss every inch of me."

I lean in close and hear his breath hitch. "Maybe if you don't disappear in the middle of the night, I could make it happen."

He pulls back and looks at me, but the fire has slightly dimmed in his eyes. "I told you, there's been, uh, stuff going on at the bar."

I know he's lying to me. "Oh, yeah?"

He knows I don't believe him.

He's known me long enough to read me. Especially because I'm not trying to mask feelings at all. I'm sure my face is obvious.

"I know I've been busy, but tonight I'm all yours."

I try not to get excited because I don't want to be let down, but I'm not quite able to completely squash the hope out of me. I've been craving him since our night. That's a lie. I've been craving him for *years*.

It might sound desperate, but I'll take anything he'd give me.

"What exactly does that mean?"

His eyes drop to my lips before he looks deep into my eyes. "It means that you and I are leaving here together and spending the entire night in each other's arms. Fucking, cuddling, you name it. We can do anything you want as long as I can have my hands on you."

I swallow the thickness in my throat and stare into his eyes. I see desperation in them. It's probably the exact look I have in mine.

"Your place or mine?" I don't care where we go as long as he does as he says and has his hands on me for the rest of the night.

"Your place is closer," he says with a panty-melting smile. I lean in, about to whisper exactly what I plan to do to make him feel better, when my brothers walk in carrying a plate of steaks and grilled potatoes.

Hudson and I pull away, but I shoot him my most seductive look, doe eyes and all. His eyes darken, and he shakes his head in response.

We all dish up and start eating. The meat is cooked to perfection, juicy and tender.

For several minutes, the only sound in the room is the clinking of forks against plates. The guys are ravenous from working all day and barely catch their breath as they scarf it down.

"You guys are animals," I say under my breath.

"Hey, we're growing boys, we have to get the proper nourishment." Cash mocks offense.

"Yeah, growing boys," I roll my eyes and tap my stomach.

"Well, now that's just mean, Del. I thought you were the nice one," Emmett says sarcastically.

"Yeah, just for that," Cash starts. He reaches across the table and stabs the remains of my steak and drags it over to his plate.

"Hey!" I yell in protest, but am met with laughter from around the table. I shoot them all daggers.

After a while, we migrate to the living room. The spring air is too crisp this time of night, or we would have gone outside to watch the sunset, but we settled for some good old-fashioned *Family Feud*. We get really into the game. There's usually yelling and mild profanities, but it's all in good fun.

Several rounds later, the sun has long since set. Doors and windows have been closed, and blankets have been passed around.

I'm sandwiched between my brothers on the couch but have a perfect view of Hudson, who's sitting in the chair diagonally from us. Cash's dog, Connie, is curled up at his feet, snoring contentedly.

"Okay, what's the score?" Cash asks. Every time we get a word on the board, we get a point.

"Del and Cash are tied with twelve. Hudson's at ten. I have six, and Emmett has four," Beck reads from his nerdy notepad. Out of all of us, he's the most organized. Or anal. I think that's a much more accurate term.

"How is that possible? I've been doing so well. You have to be cheating!" Emmet throws his hands in the air.

Beck looks down at his note to hide his face, but I see the smirk pulling at his lips. "No, you're just bad at this."

"Fuck you, what's my real score?"

Mask back in place, "Four, just like I said."

"You're such a dick. Can't win on your own, so you have to tear me down and make me look stupid."

"You're about to cry over a game. I'd say you're making yourself look stupid all on your own."

He pushes off the couch and yells, "That's it!"

Beck stands up too. "You wanna take this outside? Over your lackluster *Family Feud* performance?"

They look like they're going to tear each other apart. Each flexing their jaw and standing their ground.

Then, as I predicted, they break out in laughter. It's good to see Beckett smiling. It's been a rare occurrence recently.

We all join in on the laughter until there are tears in our eyes.

A sharp ringing breaks through the air. We all look around, reaching into our pockets to see if it's our phone.

It's not mine, so I relax back into the couch, pulling the blanket up to my chin.

"What?" Hudson's voice is stern as he holds this phone up to his ear. His eyebrows pull together, and his lips form a grim line.

He listens to the voice on the other end while the lines in his face tighten. His eyes shoot to mine before he speaks. "Yeah, just hold on. I'll be there in twenty minutes. Just wait."

I feel my face fall. It's happening again. I'll spend another night alone, and Hudson will be god knows where, with god knows who, doing god knows what.

He throws his jacket on and shoots me apologetic eyes. I look down at the floor, too disappointed to look at him.

I wait for the click of the door before I raise my eyes again.

My skin is hot. Not in the tingling way Hudson normally makes it, but hot out of the rage coursing through my veins.

I throw off my blanket and huff out a breath. He lied to me.

After ditching me all week, lying about being busy at the bar, and now running out on our plans, I'm done.

I may want Hudson more than I want my next breath, but I will not allow him to treat me as if I'm expendable.

I'm what he should be working so hard towards. What's taking up his time. I don't deserve to be an afterthought, and I will not allow him to treat me as if I am.

Screw him, and screw this. I'm going home.

Chapter Fifteen

Hudson

I'm fucking this up bad.

The look in Delilah's eyes when I was on the phone was enough to rip my heart out of my chest. She looked devastated.

Worse than that, she looked as though she felt rejected. By me.

Which is as far from the truth as it can be.

I want that woman more than I want the blood in my veins to continue flowing.

I've wanted her for years and the second she's in reach I fuck it up.

No. I haven't fucked it up. My dad has fucked it up.

He's been a real bender this last week.

At the bars from open to close.

Or more appropriately, open till he gets kicked out.

There's a town up north called Copper Falls that hosts, wait for it, dog racing. And no, it's not what you're thinking. It's not a bunch of underfed and overworked greyhound dogs running around a track. This dog racing includes a week of festivities. For seven days, a different breed of dog races in a one-hundred-meter dash.

Day one is wiener dogs, my personal favorite. They start at one end and take their sweet time sauntering to their owner at the other end.

It can take ten minutes for all the dogs to get to the finish line, but the audience waits for them eagerly with bated breath and cheers to the moon when the last dog finally crosses the line.

Some of the dogs wear glittery costumes or jingle bell collars to boost the cheering squad.

It's been going on for decades, but has only gained popularity as time went on. The last five or so years, the event has been tclcviscd.

Now, a normal person sits down and watches the adorable corgis and chihuahuas skip down the track. They laugh when they trip and cheer when they get back up.

My father, on the other hand, is not a normal person.

He'll find any reason to gamble. Adorable dog races included.

He goes off the wall this time of year, betting on the dogs and celebrating his win or mourning his loss for the rest of the day and night.

I've been called to come pick him up from the bar for nearly seven days straight.

That's why I've been away from Del.

It's killed me to stay away, but I don't want her to know the truth. I told her there's been trouble at the bar, but I know she knows it's a lie.

I just can't bring myself to tell her the truth.

That I've had to mop my dad off the floor every night this week because he's mourning his loss over golden retrievers racing.

It's too absurd to be believable.

I don't think she would care if I'm being honest. She's not sheltered from how the world works. She knows not everyone lives a fairytale.

But with Del, I like to pretend.

I don't want to be the one she pities or tries to fix, so I pretend to have everything under control.

I don't want to burden her with this.

She doesn't deserve that.

She also doesn't deserve to be lied to.

Which is precisely what I'm doing.

Fuck!

I can't lose her, especially after I just got her.

I should be with her this minute. Holding her naked body tight to my chest as she sleeps deeply in my arms.

I should be pressing soft kisses to her shoulders as she nuzzles into my neck.

But how can I just leave my dad? I mean, he's my dad. It's my job to take care of him. I just hate that I'm hurting Del in the process.

As soon as the sun's up, I'm going to get my girl. I can't go any longer knowing she's angry with me.

I could see the hurt in her eyes when I left so abruptly last night. I want to scrap that look away and make sure I'm never the cause of it again.

Tearing my shirt over my head, I flop myself into bed. I need a few hours of sleep before I go see her.

Spring is always the most challenging time on the ranch. Catching up after the winter months and starting anew is exhausting work. Then I've been up every night dealing with my dad. I'm running on fumes, and I need to reset myself before I apologize to her.

Because that's where I'm going to start.

With an apology.

Chapter Sixteen

Delilah

I gave a few samples of my new *blue peach* jam to my regular vendors and got raving reviews.

Nearly every business I work with has placed an order for a large quantity of the stuff.

The problem is, I don't have nearly enough blueberries to make all that jam.

I need to go and stock up, so I'm heading out to Sugarbush Forest. That land is hundreds of acres of woods sprinkled with the occasional hunting cabin. In the fall, it's way too risky to be out in the woods because of the hunters, but the spring is entirely safe.

Most people don't know this, but about ten miles off the last gate on the road is a patch of blueberry bushes so dense you risk getting lost in them.

I found them when I was a kid, and my dad took us all out to teach us to shoot. None of us picked it up for sport, but I found the bushes that fuel my business, so it was worth it.

I've deemed it a blueberry haven and unofficially call it my own.

I'm hoping to pick about one hundred pounds of blueberries. Enough to fulfill my orders and have extra for the off-season.

I will probably come back later in the summer to get another batch, but I can only do so much at once.

It may seem easy, but hunching over the bushes for hours on end is exhausting. By the end of the day, my back is killing me, and my fingers are numb. Then, I sleep on the hard ground and wake up to do it all over again.

That's the easy part.

The hard part is loading the five-gallon buckets into my truck bed. That's the part I always wish I had help with.

Throwing my duffle into the back seat of my pickup, I head around to my shed to grab my buckets.

I pound on the door a few times to scare the squirrels away and head inside, stacking the buckets up and rolling them into the driveway.

I like to give them a good wash before I fill them with fruit, so I head around to the side of the house and spin the faucet. The metal squeaks as it grinds together, and an ice-cold stream starts to flow from the handle and onto my hand.

I unwrap the green garden hose and drag it down my gravel driveway, kicking pebbles up in my wake.

Then, I line the buckets up and give them a spray down.

I start to sweat from the sun beating down on me, so I plug the hose with my thumb and angle it upward into the air, causing a light mist to rain down on me.

The cool droplets ease the burn on my skin, and I tip my head back to savor the feel of it.

"Don't you have a shower inside?" Even though I'm pissed, his voice triggers a carnal reaction in my body. My skin heats, my heart pounds, and that secret spot between my thighs starts to tingle.

I will my body to loathe him the way my mind currently does, but it isn't cooperating.

I turn to look at him and fix a scowl on my face. "I'm surprised to see you," I say sarcastically. "Honestly, I assumed you'd be anywhere but with me, considering you can't give me the time of day."

I may be exaggerating the situation a bit, but I'm angry and I want him to know that. I'm mad at him for ditching me, and even more enraged at myself because of the excitement I feel that he's here now.

"That's not true and you know it."

I roll my eyes and start dragging my hose back to its hook on the side of the house. The faucet is still on, so water drips down my legs and onto my muck boots.

"Look at me," he commands. It'll be a cold day in hell before I let the deep timbre of his voice distract me again.

I pick up my pace and make it to the side of my house. I crank the faucet off and roll up the hose. Then, I wipe my dirt-flecked hands across my thighs and spread the mud down my jeans.

Walking back to my driveway, my eyes widen as I see him still standing there, staring at me. There's a dark hint to his gaze, and I can't help but shiver.

I seem to be frozen to my spot. He takes a slow, deliberate step closer. My throat works, and goose bumps rise on my skin as he nears.

I want to tell him to turn around, get in his truck, and get the hell off my property. But, there is a magnetic pull between us that not even the most potent force in the universe could stop. I'm powerless against him.

He makes me weak in a way I resent.

"I can't do it, Hudson."

The dark intent in his eyes disappears and is replaced with... is that fear?

He takes a step back and raises his arms in surrender. "Don't do this. Please." He sounds so sad. Hudson is always level-headed and calm, so this is unlike him.

What does he think I'm doing?

I'm trying to protect my heart before he smashes it on the ground and runs over it with his truck.

That's what I'm doing.

"Do what?" His eyes are wide and pleading.

Hesitantly, waiting for my answer, he raises his hand to my face. His eyes search mine, and I subtly nod my consent. His rough hand gently caresses my jaw, and he brings his body closer.

My heart beats so fast I feel unsteady, but I know he'll catch me if I fall.

"Don't walk away from me." It's a demand, but it's laced with desperation.

"You are the one who is constantly walking out the door. Not me." I feel the fury rising to the surface. Despite his steady breathing and easy touch, I still feel the urge to scream at the sky. "I will not be there when it's convenient for you. I deserve better, and you know it."

I want to beat my fists against his chest.

His stupid, muscular, warm chest.

Damnit! I'm pissed! Why won't the maddening thoughts stop?

My feelings for him at this moment are nothing short of a paradox. I want to run far away in the opposite direction and have him hold me in the next moment.

He angles my eyes up to his. "I'm so sorry, Del."

I don't know why, but his words surprise me. Men aren't known to regret their actions, but the pain in his voice is unmistakable.

"I have dreamed of calling you mine since I understood the concept. Probably before, if I'm being honest," He shrugs a shoulder, his thumb traces soft circles on my cheekbone, and I feel myself melting into his words. "I remember the first time I saw you. I was twelve years old, and you came running up to me, covered in dirt with a fistful of carrots. You demanded my friendship and grabbed my hand. In that moment, my fate was sealed. My soul was forever tied to yours. You claimed me all those years ago, and I have been bound to you since."

His words fill the cracks of his rejection, yet I do not allow myself to forget the way he treated me since he *got* me.

"Your words and actions do not align." I feel physical pain, and I step away and out of his reach. My skin feels chilled at the loss of him.

I push my feelings down and walk past him, tossing my buckets into the bed and slamming the tailgate shut.

"Let me make it up to you!" He all but yells at me. I spin to face him.

He looks frantic as he walks up to me, stopping a few passes away, allowing me the illusion of space. Anytime I'm in his vicinity, I'm wholly consumed, unable to think rationally.

"Let me go with you! You and I will be alone for days with no distractions or interruptions. Please. I need you to know the depth of my devotion."

I scoff. His words are grand, but his actions do not confirm them. "If your words were true, I would feel them, and you would not need to divulge them so desperately."

I'm being unfair. I can tell he is otherwise occupied, but that does not negate the fact that I'm not being treated fairly.

If he is offering to go away with me and leave all his responsibilities, it must be a sign of good faith.

Away in the woods, there would be no choice but to say. We would arrive together and leave together. Secluded away from the world.

My mind is spinning.

Maybe it could be a good thing for him to come with me.

"Please, Del."

I'm such a sucker for him because I can feel myself relenting. I can feel my brain actively pushing his wrongdoings to the back of my mind and allowing hope to bloom in its place.

I might be screwing myself but I don't want to waste this chance.

"Fine," I say under my breath and jump into my passenger seat. If I'm gonna be stuck in the car with him for two hours, he sure as hell can drive.

He giddily jumps into the driver's side and starts the engine without saying a word. I have my gaze trained out the windshield, my attempt at giving him the silent treatment.

I feel him gaze at me and see a small smile draw on his face, before he shifts into drive and pulls onto the road. It'll be just him and me together for the next few days.

Chapter Seventeen

Hudson

O kay. I can fix this.

I managed to secure a few uninterrupted days with Del.

Very impromptu, days. I didn't have a chance to tell anybody I was leaving, so they'll just have to get on without me. My dad included.

I try to ignore the worry in the back of my mind and focus on the woman in front of me.

We drove in companionable silence, with me stealing glances at her and her forcing herself to ignore me.

The drive was beautiful and offered views of the bright green leaves forming on the trees and patches of young wildflowers.

Once we arrived, she promptly took off to form a plan for her day of berry picking and left me to set up the tent and start a fire at the campsite.

After what feels like hours of guesswork staking the tent to the earth, I arrange some logs and light them with a match. They start to crackle, and their labor echoes through the lonely forest.

The sun is on its last dregs of the evening, a deep orange painting the sky, and reflects its twin light of the fire.

The minutes of daylight are waning, and I don't want Delilah alone in the middle of the woods once that happens.

After walking in the same direction she took off in, I call out her name. The word bounces off the trees and sends the bird soaring into the air.

My steps grow in speed the longer she doesn't reply.

I call out again, and my breathing picks up speed.

What if she's lost? What if something gets to her?

"Del!" I call her name a few times in succession. "I know you're pissed but I'm freaking out so let me know you're okay and then go back to the silent treatment!"

I hear a twig snap, and I spin around to come face to face with her. Her chest is rising and falling with labored breaths, much like mine.

"I went back to the campsite and you weren't there!" She marches up to me and fists my shirt in her little hands. "Why the hell are you all the way out here? You scared me!"

I pull her in for a hug and feel her heart rate slow the longer I hold her. "I was looking for you," I whisper.

She moves her hands to my back and squeezes me tight, her nails digging into my muscles.

I wrap my free hand around her nape and angle her head back so she's looking at my face. "I'm okay."

Then, I drop a lingering kiss on her forehead, letting my lips rest against her warm skin. I feel her shiver beneath my touch. "Are you ready to head back? Get started on dinner?"

She nods but doesn't make a move to step away.

"I.. I thought you left again." That simple sentence cracks my heart in two.

"I'm not going anywhere." That's a promise. "Let's go, come on."

I usher her back to the campsite, keeping my hand on her lower back the entire time.

Once we arrive, I sit her down on a camp chair and throw a blanket over her shoulders. The air is icy, and the fire isn't enough to keep her warm.

I want to pull her into my lap, but she's still a little freaked out from the woods, so I give her a few minutes to calm down and get started on dinner.

After the food is cooked, I set a plate in front of her and sit in the chair next to her with my own. We eat in silence, which stretches to an uncomfortable level. The silence makes my mind wander to places I'd rather not be.

"My dad's a drunk with a gambling problem," I blurt into the silence.

Her shoulders pull back, and she looks at me wide-eyed. "What?"

I look away from her and stare into the fire. The yellows and oranges dance together to form the most captivating show.

I can't look her in the eyes when I say this, so I just watch the wood burn. "Yeah... so, he's been having a hard time recently. That's why I haven't been around much. I've been dealing with him."

I feel her eyes burning into the side of my face, but I can't risk looking at her face. I don't want to see what's reflecting back at me.

"What exactly does *dealing with* mean?"

I huff out a humorless laugh. "It means that I'm the one the bartender calls when he's too drunk to walk. It means I have to pick him up in the middle of the night when he's lost all his money on bets and starts fighting."

She doesn't say anything, but I hear her huff out a breath.

There's some rustling next to me, and then she's standing in front of me. Her cheeks are rosy. From the cool air or warm fire, I'm not sure. She has the knit blanket wrapped around her shoulders, and the fire is casting dark shadows across her face.

She plops herself on my lap and tucks her head into my chest. I wrap my arms around her and squeeze.

The feel of her body curled into mine is euphoric. Everything feels right when she's close. When I can feel her chest rising and falling in a steady rhythm.

Her delicate smell calms the nerves I feel from this conversation.

"So that's where you've been." It's not a question, but a statement. She's a smart girl, and now that she has the facts, she'll be able to put the pieces together.

"Yes. He's kinda gone off the wall recently, and Jimmy from the bar keeps threatening to call the cops."

"Why don't you let him? Call the cops, I mean."

I brush her hair from her face and kiss her temple before murmuring against her skin. "He's my dad, I don't have a choice."

She shifts on my lap so she's looking at me. "It's not fair to you, Hudson. You're his son; he's supposed to take care of you. Not the other way around."

If only she knew. "It's never been like that for us."

"What do you mean?" She cocks her head. Then I see it click. "Hudson, how long has this been going on?"

I want this woman to be my future, and for that to happen, she needs to know the truth. I made her brothers promise to keep it a secret from her, but it's time for her to know the truth.

"I think I was about eight the first time he took me to the bar with him. He used to leave me at home, but the neighbors started threatening to call the cops. Anyway, he quickly realized I have quite the knack for pool. I never lost, even as a kid. He started betting on my games and reaped huge payouts as a result. For a couple of years, he was taking me out every night..."

I trail off because this next part might be hard for her to hear.

"Your dad figured it out, actually. He noticed that I was doing all my dad's work while he was sleeping during the day. Then he caught on to us sneaking off the ranch after everyone had gone to bed. He put the pieces together."

She's hurt. I can see it in her face. "I'm assuming my brothers know."

I nod, and her lips tighten into a flat line.

"I didn't want you to know. I... well, I was embarrassed."

"So why are you telling me now?" She doesn't sound upset, just curious.

I told myself I'm telling her the truth, so that's what I'm going to do. "I don't want to start our relationship off with secrets and lies."

She holds my face with her hands and rests her forehead on mine. "Is that what this is? A relationship."

"Yes, you're my girl," I declare and squeeze her closer to me.

"If you don't want to start off on secrets, then we need to tell my brothers." She's right, of course, but I'm not looking forward to it at all. They're definitely going to punch me, and it's going to hurt. They're big guys and they've been known to lose control when they're pissed.

"You're right, but they're going to hate me."

"Maybe for a little while, but they'll get over it." She sounds confident, but I'm not sure.

All I know is that I'll take a thousand punches for her. I'll take her brothers hating me if it means she's by my side.

"Thank you for telling me, Hudson."

"I've wanted to for a long time, I was just scared it'd freak you out." I kiss the tip of her nose. "I need you to know I wasn't staying away because I wanted to. It killed me to stay away. Every night, I dreamed about having you in my arms. About feeling your skin on mine and feeling your lips on me."

I hear her gasp. She pulls away, and I see her pupils are blown. "Maybe we can make up for lost time?" Her voice is seductively low.

She pushes to stand, and the loss of her body on mine makes me shiver. I scramble to pull her back into my lap, but she drops to her knees in front of me.

Holy fuck. Is this really happening?

Her dainty hands trace up and down my thighs as she repositions herself closer.

One of my hands is on the armrest, fist clenched as tight as I can. I bring my other hand up and twine my fingers through her silky hair at the base of her skull.

The strands are soft between my fingers, and I tighten my grip and force her to look up at me.

"You don't have to do this, ladybug."

She moves her hands even higher up my jeans to my hips and dips her fingers under my waistband. My skin tingles at her touch and I feel my cock straining against my jeans.

"Please, let me." She begs so beautifully, and I can't resist her. Not that I want to. I've spent many days imagining what she'd look like on her knees for me, and let's just say none of them come close to the actual thing.

"Go ahead then baby, take my cock out."

She listens so well, opening my button and pulling the material of my jeans down. I help her work them over my hips until my cock springs free.

"Woah," she breaths and every spare drop of blood races to my cock. "You're huge." She takes it in her hand and gives me a tentative pump. "There's no way this thing will fit inside me."

I chuckle and stroke a piece of hair behind her ear. "We'll start slow, baby. But, eventually, you'll take every inch."

"I don't think that's going to be possible," she says under her breath.

She hasn't taken her eyes off my cock since she took it out. I love the attention, but I need her focus right now. I use my grip on her scalp and force her to look at me. "Trust me, Del, I'll have your pussy aching for me. You'll be so desperate to have my cock inside you, you'll be begging for it."

"That, I believe. I just don't know how it's going to fit." She's still stroking me slowly, and I'm about ready to lose it.

"It'll be okay, ladybug. I won't give you anything more than you can handle. I promise you'll enjoy it."

She nods her head. Her soft blue eyes are gazing at me like I hold the key to all her desires.

"Now, be a good girl for me and put my cock in your hot, little mouth."

I loosen my grip on her hair and allow her to move freely.

She wraps her lips around my tip, and I swear I tremble.

I have never felt anything so good, and she's barely touched me. I need to pull myself together before she gets the wrong impression.

But, damn.

She rolls her tongue around my tip and stars dance behind my eyes.

"Fuck," I groan. Her eyes flick up to mine, and I'm done for. The girl of my dreams on her knees for me, looking at me with doe eyes as my cock stretches her mouth.

Yeah, my fate is sealed.

Maintaining eye contact she moves her mouth farther down my cock, using her tongue for friction.

She bobs her head up and down, rolling her tongue over my tip, before taking me as far as she can and using her hands to stroke my base. I throw my head back and trust my hips up.

She gags, and I immediately pull back. "Too much?"

She shakes her head but releases my cock with one last suck. "More... please. I can take it."

I can see the outline of her tits through her button down as her chest rises and falls from her heaving breaths.

She goes back to work, stroking from base to tip and then sealing her lips around me.

My groan echoes through the forest. This girl will be the death of me, and I'll gladly go if it means I get to experience this feeling for a second time.

She finds my eyes and nods, so I start to pump my hips, matching her rhythm. Slowly, I increase my thrusts until I'm dictating the speed and guiding her head to take me just the way I want.

I don't push her too hard. We will have plenty of time for her to learn to take me deeper, but for tonight, I wish for nothing more than exactly what she's giving me.

She moans as I fuck her mouth and it spurs me to move faster.

Saliva falls from the corners of her lips, and she drops her gaze.

"Eyes on me," I say, and tighten my hold on her. She obeys my demand, but her cheeks are flushed with embarrassment instead of lust. I don't like that.

I slow down my movements until my cock is simply resting in her mouth. I allow her to catch her breath as I gently stroke her face.

She is the most beautiful woman I have ever, and will ever, lay eyes on. But something is bothering her. Her eyes have cleared from their lust-filled haze.

"What's going on in that head of yours?"

She looks away from me and murmurs under her breath, "I look disgusting, I don't like you seeing me like this."

To say I'm confused is an understatement. She looks ethereal. Her hair disheveled from my hands running through it, a blush painting her chest, the glow of the firelight decorating her in a golden hue.

When she uses the back of her hand to wipe the stray strings of spit off her chin, I understand.

"Oh, baby," I coo and pull her hands away from her face. "You have no idea how breathtaking you are."

"Don't lie to me, Hudson. I'm drooling all over myself." She fights my hold, but I don't let up.

I drop a featherlight kiss to her forehead and use my own thumbs to clear her face. Her eyes soften at my touch.

"Do you want to stop, my love?" I pray she doesn't, but I'd also be more than happy to tuck her under my arm and kiss her until she falls asleep.

"No, I don't want to stop." I sigh in relief. My cock is throbbing. A few more pumps and I'll be done for.

"Do you want me to slow down?"

"I've never done it like this before. I... I don't want to look like this in front of you."

"Let me tell you something," I start. "Watching you take my cock is enough to break me. You are so incredibly sexy, and seeing you literally drooling over me is my dream come true. I don't want you to feel uncomfortable, but I need you to know that seeing you like this is a dream come true."

Her smile is instant, and a tightness eases from my chest.

"Can I try again?" She asks and brings her attention back to my throbbing cock. No humor, I can actually see it pulsing.

"Only if you want to." *Please try again. Please put my cock back in your mouth.*

She puts me back in and sucks with new passion. She goes faster and deeper.

I start to move my hips, and she whimpers when I hit the back of her throat. I try to pull away, but she digs her nails into my thighs to keep me in place.

She hollows out her checks and sucks the soul out of me. Literally. Time seems to halt, and heat engulfs me.

My spine tingles and my body vibrates as I come harder than I have before.

Mind going blank, I'm overwhelmed with pleasure. My entire body vibrates as she sucks me dry.

She pulls back only when my cock starts to soften. She licks her lips, getting my come off of them, and I swear I feel another orgasm building. My come is spilling from her mouth, and she keeps searching for more.

She gasps as I frame her face with my hands and slam my lips to hers. I devour her, showing her how much she means to me.

I groan when my tongue breeches her mouth, and I taste myself on her.

Feasting on her for what feels like hours, my lips feel numb, and the chill in the air becomes harsh.

I pick her up bridal style and carry her to our tent.

Lying her down gently, I tuck her under the blankets, then join her. We snuggle under the sleeping bag, wrapped in each other's arms, and fall asleep to the soothing beat of each other's breaths.

Chapter Eighteen

Delilah

I've been coming out to this patch to pick berries since I was a teenager. I have my whole method laid out. Start in the south corner and work my way up.

This way, I can easily track my progress and hit every single patch, maximizing my overhaul.

Now, I explained my process to Hudson as we walked here. I have him starting at the far end of the row so we can connect in the middle. That way, we don't miss any berries. He nodded and asked questions, so I assumed we were on the same page.

I was very wrong.

I bet if I looked in his five-gallon bucket right now, there'd barely be enough to make eight ounces of jam.

He's acting like a little kid at his first strawberry patch.

Eating more than he's picking.

And I have proof.

The purple stains around his lips are giving him away.

"Hey, Hudson," I call out to him. His head snaps up, and he meets my gaze with a smile.

"Yes, ladybug?" I love it when he calls me that. It makes my heart flutter.

"How's it going over there?"

His eyes pop open like he's been caught stealing from the cookie jar. He looks down at his bucket, then back at me. He rubs the back of his neck with his free hand in a nervous gesture.

"Oh... well, it's going pretty well." His voice lacks conviction.

I can't help but give him a hard time. "My bucket is getting really full," I sing-song. "Are you ready to take a load back to camp and grab fresh buckets?"

I have to fight to hold in my laugh as panic flashes in his eyes. "Your buckets already full?" He sounds genuinely astonished, and I break out in a fit of giggles.

He sets his bucket down and puts his hands on his hips. His t-shirt stretching across his muscles, making my mouth water.

"Are you laughing at me?" He raises an eyebrow at me, trying to look serious, but it only makes me want to rip his clothes off.

If this day weren't about securing my product for the winter months, I wouldn't have let him leave our tent this morning. I would have spent the day devouring him, learning his body. Letting him learn mine. In all the ways we haven't yet.

But we will. And I have just the idea on how to make it happen.

"I was hoping with your help we'd finish early and spend some..." I pretend to contemplate the words, tapping my finger on my lips. "Quality time together."

His gaze darkens, and his eyes rove over my body. Today, I'm wearing a ratty set of jeans and a hoodie. Paired with elbow-high gloves to save my skin from the prickers in the bushes, yet he stares at me like I'm wearing lace lingerie from Paris.

"And by quality time, you mean..." He trails off like he's lost in thought. He licks his lips and shakes his head. "Can we take a break?"

As tempting as that offer is, I know if we do, we will not return. The minute I get my hands on him, I will not be able to remove them.

I've been waiting all my life for this moment. I can wait a few more hours. I'm confident he will be worth it.

"I need to fill all the buckets before I can stop. The faster they're filled, the sooner we can have that quality time."

It's as if a spark was ignited in him. His eyes widen for a split second before he hunches over the bushes and starts throwing berries into the blue bucket like his life depends on it.

I watch him for a few moments, working like the hounds of hell are chasing him. His fingers move so fast as he fills the bucket in record time.

It's equally heartwarming and amusing to watch him work so quickly.

I give him one more longing glance before I start a new bucket.

As the sun lowers on the horizon, a routine has been developed.

For every bucket I fill, he fills two.

Throughout my years, I have never gathered so many berries in such a short time.

When the crickets start their melody and the whisps of night dance on my skin, I look up to see Hudson standing next to me with a pantie-melting smile.

"All done, baby." He grabs me by the waist and softly kneads my flesh. "I filled all the buckets you had in the truck! Can we have that *quality time* now?"

He's giddy. Balancing on the balls of his feet and rubbing my soft skin with his fingers.

"I am rather impressed with how fast you filled those buckets, baby. I think you deserve a reward."

Fire flickers in his deep brown irises.

"Say that again," he demands, squeezing me tighter.

"You deserve a reward," I whisper in my most sultry voice. I've never used it before, so I'm taking a chance by using it now.

He steps closer. So close that I can smell the blueberries he ate on his breath.

"Not that. Call me baby again."

I take a step closer, devouring the space between us. My lips graze the stubble on his jaw before I whisper, "Take me to bed, baby. Please."

I'm not sure if it's the pet name or the please, but he scoops me up in his muscular arms, one underneath my knees, and the other supporting my back. He presses me to his chest and drops a kiss to my forehead.

Then we're moving. He's marching the short distance from the fruit patch back to our campsite, using his forearm to push branches out of the way so nothing hits me.

I can't help but feel giddy thinking about what's about to happen.

He sets me down outside our tent and holds the flap open for me. I bend down to crawl inside, but yelp when a swift smack cracks down on my ass.

I look over my shoulder and find Hudson staring as my ass. "Like the view?"

"Oh, Del, you have no idea. But I'm about to prove it to you."

He joins me, kneeling on the mess of blankets and sleeping bags.

Using both hands, he grabs his shirt at the waist and pulls it over his head, exposing his taunt abs that stretch with the movement, and I reach out and drag my fingers across them. They tighten and quiver under my touch.

He throws his shirt to the side so he's naked from the waist up. I want to run my tongue over his stomach and chest, then bite the muscles on his arms.

"You're staring, Del."

"Can you blame me?" I ask sarcastically without taking my eyes off his beautiful body.

His jeans rest low on his hips and I can see the stretch of hair leading to his cock.

I remember how big it is, how he stretched my mouth wide open last night, and have a moment of panic.

It's going to hurt so bad.

But maybe I want it to.

I want to feel him stretching me wide. Feel him forcing my body to accept him.

And it will. Accept him.

I've been absentmindedly dragging my fingers across his exposed chest. I do one more pass before I stop at his waist and dip my pointer fingers under that waistband of his jeans.

His body quivers, and I look up to see that his pupils are blown wide. His eyes are always dark, but right now they look absolutely black. Like a starless night sky.

I hold eye contact while I work the button of his jeans, but he gathers my wrists in one of his hands and moves them to the side, stopping me.

"Slow down," he commands, "I want to see you."

Eager to oblige, I pull my hoodie over my head and throw it next to his discharged shirt. Then, I reach for the t-shirt I have on, but he beats me to it. He slowly pulls it up. Inch by inch, exposing my stomach, then my ribs. Then he lifts the material over my chest, exposing my breasts to the air.

My nipples pucker the second the air hits them, and Hudson groans appreciatively before disposing of the remaining material.

"Fuck, look at you." His voice is gravelly.

He starts slowly, putting his hands on my waist and dragging them up my sides. Goosebumps break out on my skin in the wake of his touch. The chill makes my nipples tighten even more.

They're aching painfully. I push my chest forward in a silent plea for a reprieve only he can offer.

He clicks his tongue in a mocking reprimand, but moves his thumbs to circle the area around my nipple. Just out of reach for me to feel any stimulation, but close enough that the ache increases.

At this point, I'm panting. My chest heaving up and down in anticipation of his touch.

I let out a whimper as he pinches both my nipples between his thumbs and forefingers. He rolls them gently, igniting sparks in my pussy.

I can feel my wetness soaking my panties and every touch he delivers to my nipples sends zings to my clit.

"Hudson, please. I... I need more." My clit is throbbing painfully, my pussy clenching on nothing.

He tsks, "Patients, baby. I want to worship every inch of your body. Starting with these beautiful tits." He kneads them in his rough hands, the calluses creating a delicious burn on my raw nipples.

He leans me backwards until I'm lying on my back and he's propped over me on his hands and knees.

Pressing kisses down my sternum, he gently nibbles on the skin.

"Hudson," I whine and twine my fingers through his hair. I try to guide his head down, but he holds firm.

He runs the flat of his tongue over my nipple, and my back arches into him.

He sucks and nibbles, switching between each one until I'm sure I'll come without him ever touching my pussy.

Then, he pulls back and looks down at me. I use my hold on his neck for leverage and wiggle, trying to get some friction.

His body stiffens and his voice is deadly low as he asks, "What the hell is this?"

180

He's looking past my breasts, and I freeze when I realize what he's staring at.

Shit!

What was I thinking?

I had always hoped this day would come, but I never truly believed it would.

"Is that what I think it is?" His jaw is tight, and the grip he has on my waist turns painful.

He's burning daggers into the four-leaf clover I got tattooed on my ribs, right next to my boob.

"Hudson, please," I rub my hands over his shoulders in an attempt to soothe him. "I had just turned eighteen, and I was head over heels in love with you. At the time, it was my way of being close to you. It was stupid. Please don't freak out."

"Don't freak out?" His voice is low. Menacing. I shiver for an entirely different reason now.

With a softness opposing the look on his face, he rubs his thumb over the clover tattoo. He's so slow. Soft. His touch feels reverent.

"You mean to tell me somebody saw you that close to your boob? Some *touched* you there? They put our symbol on your skin?"

Wait... What?

I thought he was going to freak out. It's a bit strange to see a memento of yourself on someone's skin. I was young and dumb, but I honestly never believed he would see it. It was a way for me to feel close to him, the only way I knew how.

"I... um, yes, someone tattooed me."

He groans and buries his head in my neck. "The idea of someone seeing you like this burns my soul."

"You know I've done this before, right? I'm not some chaste town girl."

"Please, don't remind me." He trails his nose down my jaw to my neck and places a soft kiss there. "You're mine. I don't want anyone else to see, let alone touch you."

"So, you're not freaked out about the tattoo?"

He chuckles along my skin. "I only wish I had seen it sooner. Then, maybe we wouldn't have had to wait so long to be together."

Then, his lips are on mine. Devouring me. Tying my soul to his.

He kisses my lips, my nose, my jaw. Down my chest to my breasts, and then my tattoo.

He spends a lot of time there, kissing and sucking. As if he wants to confirm it's truly there.

After I can't take it any longer, I pull his face up to mine and look him in the eyes. "I have been waiting a long time for this, but I can't wait any longer. I need you to fuck me."

I swear his eyes roll back in his head as his groan meets the air. "That's the sexiest thing I've ever heard, ladybug."

He pulls my jeans and underwear off, along with his own, until we're naked, chest to chest. Searching the pockets of his discharged jeans, he pulls out his wallet and produces a condom that he rolls on.

Using his hips, he nudges my knees apart and lines his cock up to my entrance. I feel my wetness coating him as he rubs my clit with his tip.

"You're so fucking wet for me."

I gyrate my hips on him, desperate for more friction. Never in my life have I felt such a desperate need for release. My clit aches and my low belly pulls tight.

He cups my jaw and holds my face close. Our foreheads rest together, and our panting breaths mingle.

I feel him stretch me as he slides inside. But when I wince, he slows.

"Shh, it's okay, baby." He snakes his hand through my legs and presses his thumb to my clit.

Sparks travel down my legs and up my arms from the new sensation.

He pushes in deeper, slowly pulling out before pushing in farther than before.

After a few shallow thrusts he goes deep and I screw my eyes shut, the stretch becoming too intense.

My nails dig into his back, creating roads of struggle.

"It's too much. I can't take it."

He stops his movements but doesn't pull out of me. "Look at me, baby."

I open my eyes and immediately relax when I see him. His eyes are hooded in pleasure, and his lips are swollen from my kisses.

My muscles relax, the tension easing from my body. "That's my girl. Keep looking at me, okay?"

I do as he says, and this time, when he thrusts to the hilt, I accept him greedily.

My legs band around his waist so I can meet him thrust for thrust.

We work in perfect harmony. Me arching at the perfect moment to take him as deep as possible. Him rolling his hips in the ideal way to hit the spot inside me I didn't know existed.

The muscles in my stomach clench painfully, and a numbness spreads through my limbs.

I feel like my mind is in another plane.

"I... I need... Hudson, it's too much." My words echo in my ears.

"You can take it, baby. You're doing so well. Taking my cock like you were meant for me."

A bead of sweat trails down his temple, and his muscles spasm as he continues to pound into me.

The pressure becomes too much, too powerful. I feel myself growing tense, but when I look up and see his inky eyes staring at me with the most profound emotion a person can hold, I relax and allow myself to fall.

He rubs slow, deliberate circles on my clit and my resolute vanishes. A scream tears out of me, echoing through the trees outside.

My legs tremble, and my nails tear across his back. For a few seconds, my reality is altered. The world I know has vanished, replaced by a hazy warmth.

He transcends me to a new existence.

I have never come so hard in my entire life. I didn't even know a release could be so powerful.

Hudson's thrusts become harsh and sloppy as he buries his head into my neck and groans harshly. The muscles in his legs quiver, and my core floods with his essence.

I am hit with aftershocks as his warmth floods me.

He gives a few more half-hearted thrusts before he collapses on top of me, nuzzling my neck and pressing adoring kisses on my face.

"Are you okay?" He pants. His breathing is labored, matching mine.

"I've never felt like this before."

I feel his cock twitch back to life inside me, and I kiss him in response.

"Fuck, baby. You have no idea what you saying that does to me."

"Yes, I do. I can feel it," I giggle.

He slaps the side of my ass and we both laugh. He's been my best friend for as long as I can remember. I'm thankful that as our relationship evolves, we will always have the foundation of friendship.

After a few minutes of giggles and gentle kisses, he pushes onto his forearms and pulls his cock out of my sensitive pussy. I wince, and his eyes grow wide with worry.

"Fuck, Im sorry Del." He looks regretful, "I should have been gentler."

I push his hair off his forehead and kiss the tip of his nose. "You were perfect. You're just big and I need to get used to you."

"If you weren't sore, I'd be helping you acclimate to me all night long."

As much as I want him to fuck me until the sun comes up, my poor pussy cant take any more tonight. He knows it too because he takes a soft cloth from my backpack and gently cleans my thighs and pussy.

I moan as he drags the material across my tender flesh.

Once he has finished tending to me, he places a trail of kisses up my body. Then, he lies down next to me and pulls me flush against him.

Our breathing has evened out, but our hearts still beat in an erratic melody.

As he traces the outline of my body with his fingers, I feel soothed and feel myself growing tired.

My eyes drift shut, my brain shutting off. The last thing I feel is his hard body against my soft one and his lips against my ear whispering, "I'm never letting you go."

Chapter Nineteen

Hudson

The last few weeks have been nothing short of a dream come true.

Delilah and I have been inseparable.

I stay with her all night, leave for work, and come right back. I just can't be away from her without feeling like something is missing.

I haven't been back to my apartment since our adventure into the woods. Well, I went to grab some clothes from my apartment, but Del was with me and we had to take a break so I could watch her come undone beneath me.

She is breathtaking.

I want to spend every day for the rest of my life watching her fall apart for me.

We decided we're going to tell her brothers about us at the end of the week, but for now, we're simply enjoying each other.

To say I'm apprehensive would be inaccurate. I have a pretty good idea of how that conversation will go.

Three men yelling, one woman furious, and one man with several black eyes, lying on the floor.

Quite honestly, I'm surprised we have managed to stay quiet for this long.

I'm bursting at the seams, ready to tell anyone who will listen that Delilah is my girl. Make it known to anyone and everyone that she is unavailable. I don't want anyone thinking they have a chance with her, because they don't.

And it's not only that I want people to know that she's mine. It's more that I'm incredibly proud of her and want to brag to the world that I'm lucky enough to be the one going home with her.

I suppose we must credit that we have so rarely left the bedroom in the past few weeks to the fact that our relationship is still a secret.

When I'm at work with her brothers, I feel the words burning in my chest. I want them to know. I need them to know that I have loved her since we were children. That I will take care of her for the rest of our lives. That I will protect her with my life.

I know their brains will automatically assume the worst. That I have tarnished their baby sister and am only out for a fleeting moment of pleasure.

But that couldn't be further from the truth.

They're in the dark about the fact that I have waited nearly twenty years to hold her in my arms. I have hidden my true feelings for her for so long out of fear of their repercussions, but I will not stay quiet for much longer.

I'm the one who has been pining after her. Waiting like a loyal dog for her to look in my direction.

Well, she finally saw me, and I would risk anything to keep her.

Even her brothers' friendship.

Does that make my a shitty person?

Maybe, but I'll gladly wear that name tag if it means I can have my Del.

They will learn to accept us.

For her sake.

They might hate me for the rest of our lives, but eventually they will learn to pretend for her.

There is a soft rain this morning while I ride out to check on the cattle, and my jacket is decorated with tears of the earth.

Lucky is damp as I rub a hand down his neck and give him a good scratch near the base. He snickers, and I move to his other side.

"Does that feel good, buddy?" He waves his head around and peeks over his shoulder at me.

"I know, I'm cold too. We can head home, and I'll get you a blanket. Can't have my boy catching a chill, now, can we?"

"You can't be talking to yourself in the middle of a field. Someone will think you're crazy." Beckett rides up next to me and looks at me from under the brim of his hat. His henley shirt is plastered to his body from the rain, but he seems unbothered as usual.

"I'm not talking to myself," I feign offense. "I'm talking to Lucky. Not my fault your horse doesn't like you enough to have conversations."

"You're such an odd guy. Horse and I are perfectly fine without talking about our feelings and whatever."

I groan and lean my body back in the saddle. "Dude, you cannot call your horse *Horse*. He needs a real name."

"That *is* his name," he says flatly. "You haven't been around much lately."

That's the thing about Beck: he uses very few words, and when he does speak, he makes statements that demand input.

"I've been taking care of some things." I try to be vague without opening the floodgates. Del asked to be there when her brothers find out, so I've refrained from telling them.

"Everything going okay with your dad?" Nearly all the troubles in my life have been related to my father, and the Walton boys are familiar with all the gritty details.

Since our return from the berry bush, I haven't gotten a call from my father or any bar staff in a fifty-mile radius. I'm not sure if that's a good or bad thing, but I haven't been very concerned with him lately.

I have been so cocooned in the love-filled haze that is Delilah Walton that I have been unable to concern myself with his whereabouts or condition. It may sound harsh, but for the first time in my life, I don't feel like the parent in our relationship.

I feel happy, and I thank Delilah for that.

"Everything is better than it has been in a long time."

He smirks at me with knowing eyes. I'm not sure what exactly he knows, but there is a distinctive glint in his dark irises.

"I'm glad to hear it. I'll see you and Lilah this Sunday."

Then, as quickly as he arrived, he leaves. Clicking his heels into his horse's side, he rides through the mist in the direction of home.

I'm not sad to see him go, because it means I can ride straight to Del and warm up from the rain in her bed.

Yes. That sounds like an excellent idea.

There is a fire burning in her fireplace when I walk in the door—the wood crackles, sending much-needed heat towards my body.

It's not raining hard out, but there's a steady mist that has prevented me from getting dry all day.

My jeans are plastered to my skin, and my shirt is holding on to me for dear life.

I took my boots off on her front steps and drained the water out of them, but I carried them in with me and have them resting on the hearth in an attempt to dry them.

My hat may protect me from the sun, but it is no match for the rain. My hair is smooth on my forehead, and I feel like a wet dog.

The worst of all of it is my trembling body. I've huddled by the open flame in an attempt to heat myself, but am having no success.

"Baby? What are you doing?" Concern laces her tone as she peeks her head out of the kitchen. Upon seeing my unfortunate position, her eyes widen, and she pads across the room in my direction.

Despite my discomfort, I can't help but notice her sexy thighs in her tiny shorts or the fact that she's not wearing a bra under her poor excuse of a shirt.

Odd. Suddenly, I don't feel so cold.

She runs her hands from my shoulder to my cheeks and tips my face up. I grab her hands and pull them away. I don't want her to get cold.

"I'm trying to warm up. I've been outside all day, and it's quite miserable out there."

She looks at me as if I have an elephant trunk hanging from my nose. "I just have to ask, is this really the best plan you could come up with?"

Her eyes are dancing with mischief, and I can't help but chuckle.

"Seriously, Hudson, you're dripping all over my floor." She stands in front of me like a mother might her unruly child and holds out her hand. "Strip. Then go change and wipe up this mess."

My mind immediately goes to the gutter. "I must say, this demanding tone is really working for me, ladybug."

She swats my hand away when I reach for her, then takes a step back and points in the direction of the bathroom. "Go," she stomps her foot in the cutest little pout.

Like the love-sick puppy I am, I walk to the bathroom and do as she says. I hang my clothes to dry and take a hot shower to warm up my body temperature.

After a few cozy minutes of the warm stream, I dry off and dress in a t-shirt and sweats. I grab a towel off the rack and head back into the living room to wipe up my mess.

The smell coming from the kitchen is positively mouth-watering, and I head towards the scent once I've cleaned the floor around the fireplace.

Delilah is chopping something on her butcher block countertop, facing away from me. I walk up behind her and wrap my arms around her waist, nuzzling my face into her delicate neck, inhaling her soft scent, and dancing my lips on her skin. She breaks out in goosebumps, and I smile against her flesh.

She leans back into my chest and glances up at me. "Did you clean up the floor?" Her voice is low and my cock hardens. Fuck, she is tantilizing.

"Yes. Do I get a reward?" I wiggle my eyebrows, and she rolls her eyes at me.

"A reward for cleaning up a mess *you* made? No, baby, but I will feed you dinner."

I couldn't care less about dinner. All I want is to scoop her into my arms and take her to bed, throw her down and fuck her like an animal. But she made me dinner, so I will sit and eat every bite. She worked hard to prepare this meal for us, and I couldn't be more grateful. I will happily be fed a delicious meal by my girl before we get to the fun stuff.

She sits me down at the table and sets a plate of steaming food in front of me. I wait for her to sit before I start eating. The food is delicious, and we eat in comfortable silence.

After we've finished our meal, I send her outside to check on our horses before we settle in for the night. The birds have resumed chirping, so I'm confident the rain has ended for the time being. Otherwise, I would have gone outside myself.

She enjoys spending time with the horses. She talks to them just like I do.

I told her that Lucky was cold, so she decided to throw one of her blankets in the dryer for a few minutes and bring it out to him.

While she's with the horses, I clean up the kitchen before meeting her on the porch. "How's my boy doing?" We walk inside, and she kicks off her boots. I carry them over the fireplace and rest them next to mine. I quite like the image I see. Her small boots next to my large ones. It causes a warm feeling to spread through me.

"Well, he and Iz are quite the pair. Resting their heads across their stalls to be close to each other. He's head over heels for her."

I wrap my arm around her slender shoulder and guide her into her bedroom. "Like father, like son."

"Did you just call Lucky your son?" Is she mocking me? I've personally heard her say she would tie Cashton to her tow hitch and drag him down a gravel road, simply because he told her Izarra was looking her age.

"He might as well be. I love him endlessly, and I know for a fact you feel the same way about Iz."

She pulls her quilt back and exposes her creamy sheets. "You're right, but there's no need to rub it in."

She climbs into bed and slips her bare legs under the sheets, patting the bed next to her. I eagerly pull off my clothes before sliding in next to her. The material is cool and chills my skin.

I pull Del close to me until she's lying half on top of me. She uses her forearms to prop herself on my chest.

Azure eyes gaze upon me with wonder, and I feel mine soften in return. I have stared into these eyes for most of my life, but in this moment, I understand that they are a metaphor for my peace. I always found solace in the blue sky. It's the calmest part of nature, and I used it as an anchor. Gazing into Delilah's eyes now, I realize that they are the same shade of blue as the most serene of skies. Unknowingly, she has been calming me for years, just like the sky her eyes were inspired by.

"You are breathtaking." My words sound raspy. I almost don't recognize myself.

Her lips touch my forehead, then my nose, then each of my cheeks. Her touch is light and delicate. Soft. I have never been touched like this before, but I would give anything to make sure it happens again.

I can feel her emotions in every kiss. Her actions speaking what her words have not.

"Oh, Del," I whisper and cup her face with my hands. I want to tell her how much I love her. How my sun rises when she smiles at me. Assure her that the rest of my life will revolve around her happiness. But, I don't.

Like her, I allow my body to speak my mind.

Our lips crash together in a melody of passion, tangling and prying while our teeth clash.

I suck her bottom lip and give it a gentle bite. She moans into my mouth, and I kiss her with a renewed fervor.

The sheets tangle as we flip. Her legs wrap around my waist as I prop myself up on my forearms.

Our breaths mingle as we pant mere inches from each other. I don't kiss her, just take a moment to gaze upon her face. She's flushed from her cheeks down to her collarbone, eyes glistening with need.

A whimper escapes her and she grinds her pussy against my hard cock.

"Is my pussy ready for me?"

She uses her grip on my neck to try to pull me down into a kiss, but I hold strong.

"Hudson, please," she cries. "I need you." Her voice is so desperate, and I'm not strong enough to deny her any longer.

I drag my knuckles down her jaw and sternum, all the way to her center.

Her hips cant at the softest touch of my fingers. I move her shorts and panties to the side and use my thumb to massage her clit.

Her breathy mewls make my cock throb painfully and I don't waist another second. After rolling on a condom, I line myself up with her entrance and look her deep in the eyes. "You ready?"

She nods eagerly, and I slam inside her, all the way to the hilt. Her scream echoes off the walls. I'm still learning her intimate noises, so I take a moment and still inside her to allow her to accommodate to me.

Her breathing is harsh and choppy, and I have a moment of panic that I've hurt her. The concern is quickly alleviated when her nails rake down my back and she moans into my neck.

She starts to wiggle her hips in an attempt to get some sort of friction. "Please, I need you to fuck me."

Her soft voice begging me to fuck her is my kryptonite.

I pound inside her with long, hard thrusts until her legs are trembling around me.

Softly, I stroke her clit which makes the rest of her body quake, but she's still holding back.

"Come for me, Del. Let me feel you fall apart on my cock." That snaps her last bit of restraint. Her inner walls spasm around me, pulling my cock even deeper inside her. She screams and buries her head into the crook of my neck as her orgasm becomes overwhelming.

I don't let up, I keep pounding until my own orgasm slips from my body. Her pussy is still quivering from her orgasm which only intensifies my own pleasure.

Keeping myself nestled inside her, I pull her body flush with mine. Nothing is separating us. In this moment, we are one.

Only after our breathing has slowed and our heartbeats settle do I pull away and admire the beautiful pool of tears that has gathered in the corners of her eyes. If it weren't for the look of complete contentment on her face, I would be concerned.

"Are you okay? Was I too rough?" I speak quietly. I don't want to disturb her post orgasmic haze.

"I have never come so hard in my entire life," she whispers.

The fuel tank of my male ego has just been filled to the brim with that singular comment.

"That's what I like to hear." I make to stand so I can get something to clean her up with, but she grabs my wrists. I stop my movement and turn to face her.

"Don't go." She looks so small wrapped up in the sheets, her tan skin a beautiful contrast to the alabaster fabric.

I reach down and cup her cheek, placing a kiss on her forehead. "I'm just going to get something to clean up your come that's leaking out of you."

"Leave it. I like feeling what you do to me."

That male pride fuel tank I previously mentioned... consider it well and truly supplied for life.

After disposing of the condom, I heed her wishes and climb back into bed, wrapping my body around hers and kissing every inch of skin I can get my lips on.

She snuggles closer, resting her head on my chest, her arms and legs entwined with mine. A sigh of contentment leaves her lips before her breathing evens out, and she drifts off to sleep.

Since I've known her, this is all I've ever wanted. To be the one she goes to for comfort.

She's always been my beacon in the darkness. It may have been unfair to put such pressure on her, but I needed her joy and sense of self to give me a reason to keep going forward.

After years of loving her from a distance, I finally have her.

I would have waited the rest of my life for this chance.

I feel like the luckiest man in the world.

She's not only trusting me with her body, but her heart.

She's lived in mine for nearly twenty years, but it feels so much sweeter living in hers.

For the rest of my life, my heart will belong to her.

Chapter Twenty

Hudson

A cold chill flashes through my body before a hard surface meets my body. I realize I'm kissing the cool oak floor of Delilah's bedroom.

Did I just fall out of bed?

It takes me a moment to get my bearings and push myself up. I'm still hazy from sleep, so I don't immediately recognize the commotion happening around me.

I hear loud footsteps, far too heavy to be my Dels. Hopefully, she's still sound asleep, and I didn't wake her up with my mortification.

Wait... if Del's not walking around, who the hell is?

As reality dawns on me that Del could be in danger. The last of my sleep-induced mind fades away, and I jump to my feet. She's still sleeping soundly in bed, and a deep sigh of relief leaves me. However, that doesn't answer for the noise I heard.

During the night, I woke and decided to check on the horses. I had to make sure Lucky was doing okay after his day in the rain.

What? He's sensitive.

It was cold when I woke up, so I slipped on a pair of sweatpants and decided to wear them the rest of the night.

I make to leave the room and investigate the rest of the house, but stop short when I see three terrifying men standing in front of me.

Beckett, Emmett, and Cashton stand with their arms crossed and fury pouring out of them.

Now I understand how I ended up out of bed. I was physically removed from it.

Fuck. This is not how they were supposed to find out. Del wanted to sit them down and have a civil conversation. She wanted it to be calm, not an ambush.

But now, I feel like the one being ambushed.

"It wasn't supposed to be like this," I sputter out and hold my hands out in surrender. "We were-" My words get cut off as Cashton punches me square in the mouth.

I stagger back and crash down on the bed. Delilah yelps as I land on top of her. I'm quick to push off of her and regain my footing.

"You okay, ladybug?" She looks past me with horror in her eyes, and I wish we could go back in time five minutes ago when we were curled in each other's arms.

"Don't talk to her," Emmet says and pulls me away from her with a firm grip on my shoulder. I fight his hold, but he doesn't relent.

"Em, let him go!" She shrieks. Of course, he doesn't listen. I'm shoved against the wall. The force of my body hitting the wall rattles the artwork she has displayed.

Delilah is on her feet and running to us. Her frantic face is the last thing I see before yet another fist connects with my face. This is exactly how I predicted our unveiling would go, yet I still feel a sense of disappointment.

These men have known me for most of my life. They should know I would never hurt her; they should trust me with her.

But they don't. And that stings.

"How could you do this to her?" Punch. "She's my baby sister." Punch.

"I waited as long as I could," I choke out.

Delilah grabs onto his arm and tries to pull him off of me, but her shoves her off. She slips due to the force and falls to the ground. For the first time since the punches started flying, I punch back.

Cashton stumbles away from me, and I rush to Dels side. She's back on her feet by the time I get to her, but I still place a reassuring hand on her back. Her countenance is devastating, and I want nothing more than to comfort her.

"What the hell is wrong with all of you?" She shouts at her brothers. "You know I've had a crush on him my entire life!"

Cash huffs and incredulous laughs. "He's taking advantage of you, Lilah, can't you see that?" He's speaking to her like she's a child, which I don't appreciate. I also don't appreciate his words, considering I love his sister and would never take advantage of her.

"I would never harm a hair on her head. Dont be a jackass." I try to sound calm, but the tension in the room makes it very difficult.

I usher Del so she's behind me, slightly guarded by my body. I don't like the anger pouring from her brothers right now, and although I know they treat her like a prized jewel, I can't stop my protective instinct from taking over.

Emmett and Cashton are in my face, staring down at me like I am the devil himself. Beckett is standing by the door frame, simply observing the show. At least he's not yelling at me. His face is entirely devoid of emotions, and I'm unable to tell where he stands on the situation.

"You're disgusting, Hudson. We've trusted you with her our entire lives. How could you do this?" That is Cashton's last words before he shoots me a look of disdain and walks out of the room.

Emmett has always been the level-headed brother in their mix, so I'm hoping I can talk some reason into him. "Please, Em. Let us explain."

"There's nothing to explain." He doesn't sound angry, per se, more disappointed. And that hurts. They're like brothers to me. It stings that they don't trust me.

Del pushes past me and stands in front of me, talking to both her brothers. "How can you possibly be upset by him and I being together?" He's always treated me well, better than you lot. And for the love of it all, he's your best friend! You know he's a good man." By the end of her speech, she's out of breath. Her chest is heaving out of anger, and I try not to notice her nipples tenting her tank top. This is not the time, nor the place.

He doesn't address her when he speaks, "You could have fucked any woman in town and you had to pick our sister? I truly thought-"

I cut him off because he is way off base. "First of all, I'm not just fucking her. We're in a relationship because we care for each other. I know it might be a surprise to you, but I have wanted this since the first day I stepped foot on your farm. I have been loving her from a distance because I was terrified not only of her not reciprocating, but also because I didn't want to lose your friendship. But I will tell you this: if you disapprove of our relationship, I will choose her. I'll choose her every time."

The whole time I'm speaking, he nods his head slowly with a stoic expression on his face. He takes a step closer to me and crosses his arms over his chest. "You'll never be good enough for her." Then he dismisses me with a look of disdain and turns his attention to Del. " Did you know his father lives and breathes the bars? He's gambled every cent he's ever earned and made his kid pick up the slack. Do you know how Hudson acquired the bar? No, well, let me tell you? He won it gambling. Like father, like son. Am I right, Hudson? I know this may sound harsh, Liliah, but one day he will become the very thing he despises, and you will suffer the consequences."

My heart cracks into a million pieces at his words, and emotion consumes me. I cannot believe he said those things. That he thinks those things. He's been my best friend my entire life, and he thinks I'll turn out to be exactly like the man who's ruined my life. I'm left speechless, mouth hanging open like a fool.

"Get out of my house." Her tone is deathly, and a chill fills the air. She has never sounded so stern in her entire life.

Emmett's eyebrows jump up his forehead, but he schools his features quickly. "I don't mean to hurt you, Del. I just want you to know what you're getting yourself into."

"No, don't play that game. You said those things to hurt him. You just tore your best friend to shreds with a smile on your face. How can you stand there with that holier-than-thou attitude while you try to turn me against him?" She takes a deep inhale before calmly saying, "Get the hell out of my house."

"I know you hold him in high regard, but he is not the man for you." Then he spins on his heel and walks right out the door.

My chest is still splintering from what he said about me.

I have spent my entire life fighting to be the opposite of my dad, and Emmett knows that. He threw every insecurity of mine in my face and used it as ammunition to get Del to hate me.

It's just Del, Beckett, and I left in the room, but I'm pretty much useless at this point. I'm frozen from shock and betrayal.

"Are you gonna fucking say something?" She screams at Beckett across the room. He's been silent throughout all of this. Watching the carnage burn.

His face is as impassive as always. Not a notch of emotion to be found.

"Get out," she says, dripping with disdain. He does as she says and leaves without a word.

I can feel the hatred for her brothers radiating in waves from her.

This is precisely what I wanted to avoid. They're her family, and I don't want her to lose them.

I didn't want her to have to choose between us. Mainly, I was afraid that I would lose. Lose her and lose the friendship I have with her brothers.

But now, I'm worried that she *will* choose me.

I cannot allow her to disown her brothers for me.

I can not and will not be the reason they are no longer in her life.

I need to fix this. I need to fix this for her. I don't care if they hate me for the rest of my life, and judging by the things they said today, they already do. Cashton's punches hurt, but Emmett's words eviscerated me.

I will figure out a way to make this right. If I have to step away from our friendship to give Del some peace, I will do that. I will bear the burden so she doesn't have to.

Chapter Twenty-One

Delilah

I managed to wait until late afternoon before giving my brothers a piece of my mind. It took every ounce of willpower I had left to stop myself from going to the farm and laying into them.

They have pulled numerous stunts over the years, but never anything of this magnitude. Not only did they try to destroy my relationship with the only man I've ever loved, but they decimated Hudson.

Cash with his fists, Emmett with his cruel words, and Beckett with his indifference.

They have all been best friends since the day he arrived on our doorstep, and their actions made it seem that it was all for nothing.

I'm less upset about their disapproval. I expected that. But the way they all but disowned Hudson is unacceptable. They spoke to him as if he were a stranger. As if he were no better than the dirt on their boots.

I spent the day fuming. Hudson took off almost immediately after my brothers walked out. He looked heartbroken and said he needed to be alone.

I didn't believe any of the lies they said about him, and I think he knows that. He was just hurt that the people he calls his brothers could speak so harshly about him.

They were shocked by the discovery of us, I know. Why they all showed up at my house, I still don't understand, but their shock is not a justification for their brutal attack against him.

Today was meant to be the day we told them. I had it all planned out. We would start with dinner, then move to the living room where we would unwind with some *Family Feud*, and when everyone was feeling relaxed, I would break the news. They would be surprised at first, but eventually realize that there is no one better for me than him. They'd then congratulate us, and we'd exchange farewells and head home, happy and content.

A bit naive in retrospect, but I didn't think it would turn out as badly as it did.

Hudson has opted not to attend our family dinner tonight for *obvious* reasons. I was tempted to stay home as well, but I needed an opportunity to express my thoughts. They cannot get away with their behavior this morning.

I took the day to calm myself down and prepare my words before driving to the farm. I was feeling sensible when I got in the truck, but as I drove up the gravel driveway and saw that big white house, I could feel the tension bubbling beneath my skin.

I told myself I would speak calmly and rationally, but I believe I have lied. When I open the front door and hear their voices, I decide that calm is overrated.

They are sitting around the table, filling their plates with food. Looks like they started without me. I don't have the capacity to evaluate that hurt right now, and I decide instead to stay on topic. Their leaving not only Hudson, but me, out of dinner can be dealt with another day.

All of their head rise when I approach the table.

"What are you doing here, Lilah?"

What am I doing here? Well its my goddamn house too, dickhead. I have every right to be here, and him questioning that is simply offensive.

I take a deep breath. "I'm here to discuss your behavior this morning. It was reprehensible, and you should be ashamed." I sound like a mother, but they're acting like children, so it's only right.

"The only one who should be ashamed is Hudson. He took advantage of you, Del. You see that, don't you?"

I'm tempted to throw a glass at Cashton's head. How dare he insinuate that I don't have enough wits to make decisions for myself? That I could only be with Hudson under pretenses.

"You are making an ass out of yourself," I say calmly. I want to be the sane one at this table.

He stands, putting his palms on the table, and leans over it. "Me? You're the one acting like a fool!"

How can he stand there diminishing my feelings? He isn't even trying to understand. "How dare you? He's your best friend!"

"He *was* my best friend."

My eyes roll of their own volition. "What's that supposed to mean? Nothing has changed, he's still the same man he was yesterday."

"No! Yesterday, he was the man I've known since childhood. *Today* he's the man who's been lying to us and sneaking around behind our backs by fucking our sister."

Losing my temper, I slam my fists against the table. The plates rattle. All eyes fall on me. "Hate to break it to you Cash, but he's been fucking me long before today!"

A bit vulgar, I know, but I couldn't keep it in. Never in my life have I wanted to discuss my sex life with my brothers, but here we are.

He blanches at the proclamation and falls back into his seat, seemingly withering at the information.

Good. At least his mouth is finally shut.

Unfortunately, Emmett takes that as his opening.

"We're just worried about you. We know Hudson isn't a bad man, okay. We just never expected this. I mean..." he chuckles. The fucker actually chuckles. "We all know you had a crush on him when we were teenagers, but we all expected you to grow out of that."

Then, and I kid you not, he starts cutting the meat on his plate. He's eating after embarrassing his friend.

He destroyed their friendship this morning when he spilled such personal information in an attempt to scare me away from him, and he's eating.

He wanted Hudson to appear like a low-life loser, and he did a damn good job of it.

I know the truth, I know his history, and it doesn't scare me away from him.

I assume my brother believed I was uninformed on the matter. Hudson only recently told me about his past, but it is unlikely they knew this.

Learning about Hudson's past only deepened my feelings for him.

I am disappointed to call Emmett my brother after he so easily tore down someone we consider family.

"How can you be so casual?"

His eyebrows jump up his forehead as he looks at me. "It's done, Del, and it's not your fault that it happened. We blame him entirely."

"Done? What exactly is done?"

"This silly little rendezvous you and Hudson have been on."

"This isn't 1813. You have no right to dictate my relationships!"

"It seems I need to. You're clearly swept up in his charm and looks, so I need to be the one to decide rationally for you."

If looks could kill, he'd be dead on the floor from the daggers I'm throwing his way. "Well, you sure are gallant, aren't you?" My sarcasm could be detected on the moon.

"I know this is not what you want to hear, but he will end up hurting you."

If they honestly think so little of him, why have they maintained a friendship for so long? If they thought him to be a reincarnation of his father, why have they called him brother for so long?

"We're just looking out for you, Del. You're our sister, and it's our job." This comes from Cash, who appears to have regained his voice.

Their words are patronizing, and I'm growing increasingly closer to a complete loss of control. I hate when people speak down to me and act as if I couldn't possibly come to a sensible conclusion on my own. It fills me with fire. Looking at the two of them with disdain, I say, "If you were truly looking out for me, you would consider my feelings in the matter."

"This isn't about feelings. It's about Hudson." It must be because they are men that they speak without reason. Absolutely no logic behind their eyes.

"How can you sit there and speak so lowly of him, as if he hasn't been a brother as close as your own flesh and blood?"

"Listen, Del," He speaks calmly. "Hudson asked us a long time ago to keep his personal life from you. We heeded his request, but understand now that it was a misstep on our parts. Perhaps if we had told you, even confidentially, you would not have fallen for him.

"On the outside, he is no different than us, but you need to know he grew up very differently from how we did. He has done things that people shouldn't have to, and although I feel sorry for the struggles he's endured... they change a person. They harden them, and I do not want you to have to experience them, too. If he falls down the same path as his father, you would be the one to suffer, and I do not wish that fate upon you."

Although I feel sadness about my brother's disapproval and lack of faith in me, I am heartbroken over their abandonment of Hudson. I wish for him never to know the words they speak of him. "If you truly believe Hudson to be the monster you make him out to be, why did you remain friends with him?"

"Him being our friend versus him being your *boyfriend* is worlds apart. You can't compare one to the other." Emmett is so calm when he speaks, it's unnerving.

"He is the same Hudson in both roles," I shout, losing my last bit of composure. "You're just pissed because you feel betrayed! You know there is no one better than him. He cares for me! He always has, and you know that! You're angry because you feel blindsided.

"One day, you will look back on this moment and realize you betrayed your best friend. You betrayed his trust and used information about his life that he trusted you with against him." My voice rises higher and higher with every word, and I finish my rant on a screech.

Cash and Em at least have the decency to look remorseful. Beck is still sitting in his seat, food untouched, watching the show. I turn all my rage onto him. "And you! How can you just sit there and listen to this? You know this is wrong. The things they've said about him are horrible, and you say nothing to defend him? They call me naive and tell me I'm unable to make a choice about my own life, and you let them. Are you enjoying this? Do you believe it to be true?"

He stares at me for a few moments, his eyes dark as the night, boring into me. He stands and walks the short distance between us. His massive frame is imposing, even though I feel no fear towards him. He leans in and whispers in my ear, low enough that no one else can hear. "Hudson is a good man, and you are capable of making choices for yourself." Then, he raises to his full height and steps back, turning his attention to the men at the table.

"Apologize to her." Then he's walking out of the room. The thuds traveling from the floor above us indicate that he has gone to his bedroom.

Beckett has always been hard to read. He is a man of few words, but he does speak when he feels it is important. I appreciate him more now than I can express.

If only Emmett and Cashton were as level headed as their older brother.

My remaining brothers look at each other like chickens with their heads cut off. Their tiny pea brains can't comprehend how Beck could possibly believe they are in the wrong. Sure, he didn't say much, but when Beckett speaks, people listen.

Though they seem unable to oblige his demand.

They look at me but say nothing. If I'm being honest, I don't care if they apologize to me, but they need to make this right with Hudson.

"I'm not apologizing," Cash breaks the silence. He sounds like a bratty, petulant child.

Emmett crosses his arms but doesn't say anything.

I'm ready to go home. I can't stand looking at them any longer.

I didn't come here seeking their approval. I simply wanted to tell them they were being the worlds largest dick wipes.

I've said my piece, but they will need a few days to think it over. They're men and can't process information any quicker.

"I didn't come here to ask for your permission to be with him. That's happening no matter what you have to say about it." They groan and make to speak, but I cut them off. "I don't care what you say about me, but you will make this right with Hudson. The things you said about him were cruel, and one day soon you will regret having said them."

I knew they would disapprove, but I didn't anticipate such a brutal reaction. Hudson and I are happy together. They need to make this right.

"If you truly hate him for this, then you need to understand that you will lose not only your friend, but your sister too. He has never been as cruel to me as the two of you were today."

I hope they hear my words as truth, because if they don't make this right with Hudson, I will never forgive them.

Chapter Twenty-Two

Hudson

I 'll admit, I have been having the pity party of the century for the past few days. After her brothers eviscerated me that morning, I have not been able to face any of them.

Not even my Del.

She has called me countless times, but I told her I need some time alone. I want nothing more than to hold her close and tell her that what they said is false. That I am not and will never be my father, but I can't look her in the eyes.

I need her comfort, but I feel like I don't deserve it.

She has allowed me my space, although begrudgingly.

The Walton brothers have been my second family for as long as I can remember. Hearing what they truly think of me has hurt me in a way I didn't know was possible.

How long have they felt this way? Have they secretly disliked me all this time, only pretending to be my friend?

Oh god. Is it pity? Have they only been my *friend* because they felt sorry for me?

What's worse: them hating me for who I am or them feeling sorry enough to fake a friendship.

Maybe it was naive of me to think they would be understanding of my relationship with Del. I thought, after all our years together, they would have seen that I'm good enough for her.

I guess I didn't consider that they see me as a younger version of my father.

I have spent my entire life trying to be better. Working so no one could see me in him.

Del was my catalyst for improving my life. Without her, I may never have experienced a life other than the one I lived as a child. Well, I suppose I owe the entire Walton family a debt of gratitude. Before my father and I moved to the farm, I assumed every father-son relationship was like ours. I didn't see how inappropriate it was for a child to be the responsible one.

My dad always told me that I owed him for everything he did for me.

I believed him until I saw the way Mrs. and Mr. Walton loved their children, and I realized something was wrong. I watched the way their family shone around one another and couldn't understand why a gray haze formed when my father and I were together.

Even after I saw the discrepancy, I still struggled to come to terms with it. I wanted what they had and thought that by putting in more effort, I would achieve it.

Unfortunately, I'm a groan ass man and still live at my fathers beck and call. He calls, I answer. It's pathetic, really, but I still yearn for a relationship with him.

However fleeting it may be.

I thought they understood this. I thought they were proud of me for how far I've come since I was a kid. It took a lot of work for me to become who I am today, and it hurts that they can't see that. They still see me as the ratty kid who hid his dad's old beer bottles in the storage barn so he wouldn't get in trouble.

I'm living in a paradox. I want Del to hold me and tell me it's all a bad dream, but the other part of me feels sick at the prospect of facing her.

Will she feel like I lied to her? Hid a dirty secret to con her into this relationship?

The thought makes bile rise up my throat, and I throw my comforter off my clammy body. I've been in bed for days, slowly morphing into the mattress.

Some may consider it hiding. I say they can bugger off.

Pushing myself out of bed, I hobble the distance to my couch before sprawling out again.

At least it's a change of scenery.

I've been planning how I'm going to approach her brothers. What I'm going to say.

They haven't come to see me, nor have they reached out via message, but then again, neither have I.

The part of my brain that yearned for an apology wished they would tell me they didn't mean any of it, but that was a foolish hope. They meant every word.

Now I find myself in a state of limbo. I want them to love me like they always have, but I know it's not an option. I also wish to have Del by my side, but without her brother's favor, that's unlikely to happen.

Since the *incident,* Del has been nothing but her usual self. Since I've asked for space, she has been messaging me with words a lover sends to another. Not that of a disgusted foe.

That gives me hope.

If only I had the courage to message her back. I'm just too scared that anything I say will change the way she feels about me.

I don't know what to do.

If this were a parallel universe and I were dating a random girl and our relationship was in strife, I would go to the Walton brothers for advice. They're who I always go to, but now that I can't, I have no one to talk this through with.

Well, that's not quite true.

There's always Henely.

But, he's still Delilah's brother. Why would his reaction be any different than the others?

Henley is my age, and out of all the guys, we were always the closest. I still consider him to be my closest friend, even though he lives in the city.

Henley is a superstar hockey player for the Windrunners team in Chicago.

I knew his life would take a different path from mine when we were in middle school. He spent all his free time on the ice. In the winter, he would play pond hockey, and in the summer, he would play at the community rink.

When we were about thirteen years old, he convinced me to join the local hockey team. I have never been more embarrassed than I was stumbling around like a child. He *literally* ran circles around me.

He, of course, thought my inability to stay upright was hilarious.

Long story short, I didn't finish the season and decided I hate hockey.

Playing, that is.

I love watching it, and having my best friend on the team makes it much more entertaining.

I try to watch every game he plays and pester him with critiques I have no business giving once it's over. He just laughs at me and tells me to stay in my lane.

We may live in different worlds now, but he will forever be my best friend. Our connection has remained strong since he left all those years ago.

I'm sure his siblings have filled him in on how I fondled with his sister. But, then again, I haven't had a message from him in days.

It's not atypical for us to go extended periods of time without speaking. We're both grown men with a lot going on. Though I am surprised he hasn't reached out since the news broke.

It leads me to believe he doesn't know.

Maybe if I tell him myself, he'll understand.

"Fuck it," I mutter and pull out my phone. Before I can chicken out, I select the call button.

It rings for several seconds before our call connects. His face takes up my screen. His hair is tousled atop his head, and it looks like he's eating something out of a bowl.

"You look like a fucking disaster," he states bluntly. "Are you sick or something?"

Okay. Very typical Henley talk.

I think I'm in the safe zone. Although I won't be for long because I'm about to tell him I'm in love with his sister.

Yes. In love.

I've been in love with her for years, so it's not scary for me to admit it. Though being able to say it out loud feels like an elephant being taken off my chest. I want to scream it to all who will listen.

"I need to tell you something," I all but blurt out.

He looks up from his cereal bowl and quirks an eyebrow. He must see the seriousness of my face because he pushes his bowl to the side and wipes the milk drool off his chin.

"Okay. What is it?" He sounds skeptical, rightfully so. We very rarely have heart-to-hearts. The two of us are usually able to sense when something's going on with the other without needing to say anything.

"I'm in love with Delilah," I all but shout at him.

His expression surprises me when he rolls his eyes and pulls his food back in front of him. "I dont want to sound like a dick, but honestly dude, that is not news to me."

My eyebrows shoot up my forehead. "What do you mean? How do you know?"

He laughs. Almost obnoxiously.

His reaction makes me queasy, like I'm on the outside of some sort of joke. "Hudson," he says in a placating voice. "You look at her like she personally carved the moon and decorated the sky with it. You treat her with a softness one would their greatest treasure. I have watched you love her quietly for *years*. This is not news to me, but I am curious why you decided to tell me now."

I'm a bit stunned. If he knew, why did he never say anything? I wish he had so that I could have been honest with Del earlier. But that's a moot point.

"They didn't tell you?" I'm shocked his brothers didn't call him immediately and tell him to forget my name.

"What happened?"

Okay, so he's in the dark. Maybe they didn't want to upset him during training. Or perhaps they didn't think he would be on our side? The mere thought has hope blooming in my chest.

I take a deep breath and give him a synopsis of the events, not skipping over any detail, no matter how small.

"They walked in on you two in bed?" He howls in laughter.

I try to hide the mortification I'm feeling, but nod in confirmation.

"Oh, Hudson," he drawls. "That is probably the worst thing that could have happened."

"Yeah, I know," I murmur.

"I'm really trying not to laugh," he says while covering his face with his hands to hide his laughter. "I just really wish I could have been there to see it."

I wish he were there too. Maybe then I wouldn't have gotten punched so many times. Or emotionally ripped to shreds. "Believe me, it was nothing I'd want to experience again."

The humor in the conversation dies instantly. "I'm sorry for what happened."

"What am I supposed to do?" I'm unsure how to resolve this, but I need to find a solution.

"Well, you know my brothers as well as I do." I thought I did, but it turns out I have been a fool. "They are protective of her. All they want is for her to be safe and happy. They also know you. The good and the bad. To them, you are as close as a person can be to blood."

I rub a hand down my face and groan. "You didn't hear them, Henley. They hate me."

"They don't hate you. They aren't capable of hating you."

"You didn't hear the things they said. They used everything they had against me. They wanted to make her hate me. Make her scared of me."

"She could never hate you, she loves you." His statement knocks the wind out of me. She hasn't told me she loves me, but I would be a liar if I said I didn't want her to. I want her to love me the way I love her. "Yes, she loves you, idiot. She's always loved you. She's loved you as long as you have loved her." The longer he talks, the faster my heart beats. I live and breathe for her love. I hate that we have lost so much time hiding from each other. I need to find a way to mend the relationship with her brothers so we never have to spend another moment apart.

He puts his palms on the table and continues. "Just love her, Hudson. And let her love you back."

"But, your brothers-"

He cuts me off mid-sentence, "They were in shock. They saw you in their baby sister's bed... I know you don't want to hear this, but they let you off easy. Anyone else would have been in the backyard already..."

"So, they didn't kill me..." I'm having a hard time seeing where this is going.

"Don't interrupt me." I points his finger at me. I roll my eyes but signal for him to keep talking.

"They're good guys, but not nearly as clever as I am." He throws a cheeky wink at me. He just can't help himself. "They need a few days to realize just how deep a grave they dug, and once they do, they will accept this. They will not be willing to lose either of you, which will happen if they try to prevent your relationship. They know you are the best man for her; they just need to wrap their little brains around the change."

I don't want to wait. I feel like a belligerent child who wants to stamp their feet on the ground, because I want to be with her for every second of the rest of my life.

I want to be the man who cares for her, who protects her, and loves her endlessly. I will be that man regardless of what her brothers have to say about it, but I don't want to lose them. I want them to know how deep my affections for her truly are.

I hope Henely's right.

No. He has to be right.

However, even if they accept our relationship, they can't take back the things they said about me, and I'm unsure if I will be able to forgive them for that.

"Where's your head at?" Concern laces his tone, and I realize I had zoned out.

"I hope you're right, that they'll accept us. I'm just stuck on what they said, how they feel about me."

His eyes get soft, and I simultaneously want to punch the look off his face and accept a big, bear hug from my best friend. Since neither is possible over the phone, I simply let him speak. "They will realize just how deeply they fucked up and will make it right. I'm sorry they were cruel; you didn't deserve that. You have been our brother since the day we met you. We all love you. They will discover they're wrong and rectify it. I have no doubt Liliah has given them a piece of her mind and jumped-started the cogs in their brains."

I don't like the idea of Del fighting with her brothers, but I'd be a liar if I said her sticking up for me didn't fill me with warmth.

Henely's right. I need to give them time to accept our relationship.

Del and I are written in the stars; there will be no separating us. But I will not allow her to separate herself from her family. I will deal with their discontent as long as she is happy.

Chapter Twenty-Three
Delilah

Hudson asked me for space, and I've been giving it to him, despite my reluctance. What I want is to be with him and tell him how much I love him and need him in my life.

Our time apart has only deepened and solidified my feelings for him. I've loved him for a long time before we finally got together. Being with him has been everything I ever wanted, and now that we're apart again, I feel like a piece of myself is missing.

I'm at an impasse right now. I want to respect his need for space, but I don't want him to drift too far.

I know my brothers hurt him; they hurt me, too. Witnessing them be so cruel to someone they love so deeply was scary.

All I can do now is make sure he knows how I feel.

That's one thing I have control over.

He needs to know that I don't believe what my brothers said. I know they don't believe it either. They were just being royal douches because they felt left in the dark.

Pathetic, really, but I understand their reaction.

It must have been shocking to find us in that way. Their sister and best friend together in bed must have been hard to see. I'm sure they felt that we were sneaking around and hiding something from them. Which we were, but we were planning to tell them. They just discovered us first.

I'm not sure if it would have gone better if we could have told them the way I wanted. Maybe it's just a wild fantasy.

And it's moot anyway. When the time came to them finding out about us, they freaked out and hurt us both.

I need to see Hudson. I'm spiraling without him. I can't stop worrying that he'll leave me to try to please them. I don't think he would, but I can't stop the thought from making a home in my head.

Would I make it worse if I sought him out? I just miss him so bad, and I need to make sure he's okay.

I've sent him countless messages telling him that I don't think anything my brothers said is true. That I miss him and want to see him. Even just to ask how he's doing. He's only answered a few times, mainly with one-word responses telling me he's doing fine and that he's not ready to see me.

My heart cracks a little more each time he dismisses me, but I haven't given up yet.

A knock on my door breaks my thoughts. I wasn't expecting anyone, considering I'm not speaking to my brothers, and Hudson has been avoiding me like the plague.

Wait... could it be Hudson?

My chest tightens with excitement, and I run to my front door and swing it open. My shoulders fall when I see Beckett standing on my front porch. "What do you want?" I can hear the grit in my voice, but I'm disappointed it's not my Hudson.

"Good to see you too," he says jokingly and sits down at one of my wicker rocking chairs at the end of my porch.

"It's not good to see you, that's why I didn't say it," I grumble and take a seat next to him.

We sit in silence for a few minutes, letting the fresh spring breeze rock us back and forth. Beck's solitary to a fault, so it's no surprise that he's as quiet as I am.

I'm not talking because I'm angry, but he's not speaking because he is a subpar conversationalist. Usually, I take pity on him and talk so he doesn't have to, but not today.

I don't think he's shy; he's always comfortable in a room. He just doesn't speak unless there's a reason to. I respect him for that because so many people never stop moving their mouths.

"It shouldn't have happened like that." He sounds genuinely remorseful, and it makes the fury inside me stir to life.

"What exactly are you trying to say?" Don't be fooled. I know exactly what he's saying. He's trying to blame me for the things Cash and Em said to Hudson. He's not going to get away with that.

He runs his fingers through his hair before settling deeply into the chair. He looks nervous, which makes me think I might be misreading this situation. "We ambushed you, and I'm sorry. You should have been able to tell us on a neutral playing field."

I feel myself jerk back at his admission. He's not blaming me. In fact, it sounds like he's trying to apologize. "We were going to tell you that night. Over family dinner."

"I figured you would be telling us soon."

Wait, what? "You knew?"

He chuckles and fixes me with a stare. "Yes, Liliah. I have known about your feelings for each other for quite some time."

It was no secret that I had a crush on him when we were kids, but as we grew up, I thought I had gotten better at hiding my feelings.

"Don't give me that face," he says, and I realize my eyebrows have furrowed in thought. "You have always cared for him, and he has always cared for you. I knew it was only a matter of time before you ended up together."

"If you all knew, then why did they freak out the way they did?" Did they all hope we would ignore our feelings forever?

"I said *I* knew. I don't think they ever suspected."

So, Beck knew the whole time. Even before we did. "What exactly are you trying to tell me?"

"I just want you to know that I'm happy for you and that I'm sorry for what's happening."

I feel instant relief at my oldest brother's approval, but that still doesn't change the precarious situation we're still in. "Thank you, Beck. Your accepting us is all we wanted, but it doesn't fix what you all did."

Now he looks surprised. "What do you mean, *what we all did*? I didn't do anything."

I puff out a humorless laugh. "You might not have said anything to hurt him, but by staying silent, you all but confirmed that you believe what they said. You didn't defend him, and I'm sure that's killing him."

"Fuck," he says under his breath. Did he honestly not think he did anything wrong? How do men survive with a complete lack of social awareness?

"I think you broke him," I whisper. It's the first time I've admitted it out loud.

He leans forward and rests his elbows on his knees. "How has he been. Since that morning, I mean?"

I can't help the inflection in my voice as I all but shriek, "You mean the morning his best friends hit him and used his deepest insecurities against him?" Obviously, I know that's the day he's talking about, but I need him to remember how horribly they behaved.

He nods sheepishly, and I continue. "Well, I wouldn't know. Considering the fact that he has refused to see me since," I say with pure malice, but I relax my tone before I continue. "I'd assume he's not doing well, considering he lost all his friends."

"What do you mean he won't see you?" He sounds shocked.

"I mean," I start slowly, "He doesn't want me around."

"I'll fix this, Lilah. I promise." His tone is laced with determination.

"I don't see how that's possible."

"He needs you."

"If that were true, he would be with me," I say sadly.

He hits me with a small smile. "You and I both know that's not true. He's torn between you and us."

"And whose fault is that?" I can't help throwing in.

"It's ours, and I will make sure to fix it, but in the meantime, you need to go to him."

"He doesn't want me, weren't you listening?" I feel myself getting angry. Hudson won't have me, and Beck's telling me that he needs me.

"He does. I'm as sure of it as I am about the sun rising tomorrow. He's staying away, so you don't have to choose. He's sacrificing himself for you."

I hadn't thought of it that way. That he's staying away so I don't have to choose between them. So I won't lose my family. The realization makes me love him more, and I can't help the choked sob that bubbles out of my throat.

"How do I fix this?"

"Just go to him, be there for him. Show him that you can have both him and us. The rest will heal itself."

"I can't lose him," I admit. I hate being so vulnerable, but I trust my oldest brother.

"You won't. The two of you are two halves of the same apple. It's Em, Cash, and I who need to mend our relationship with him."

"It'll break him to lose you all."

"He won't." He sounds so confident. He better be right and make good on his words. "Be with him now, he needs you."

He pushes himself off the chair and stops in front of me, squeezing my shoulder, offering reassurance. I watch as he gets in his truck and drives off in the direction of the ranch.

Having Beckett's support takes the weight off my chest.

At least one of my brothers is happy for me.

❋❋❋❋❋❋❋❋❋❋❋❋

I thought about what I'm going to say to Hudson all night. I want to have my words perfect so I can convince him that this whole hiatus act is no longer going to work.

I am not choosing him over my brothers by being with him. That's the main message I need to get across to him.

And, while we wait for them to make it right with him, we will be together.

The problem is, whenever I imagine us having this very important conversation, I get distracted by the Adonis that is Hudson. I can feel his phantom hands gliding up and down my skin as he looks me in the eyes and whispers lowly in my ear.

I think I'm having Hudson withdrawals.

I went a long time without having his body, but now that I've had him, I'm craving him. I need his fingers holding my flesh tight and his cock stretching me wide.

I need to focus!

First, I need to get him to accept that I'm not losing him or my brothers. Then, hopefully, we can celebrate in each other's embrace.

I gave myself the morning to gather my thoughts and make a plan, since I need to bring a jam delivery to town. After I drop off my product, I plan to stop by his house to talk to him.

Earlier, Beck told me he hasn't shown up to work at the ranch all week. If he's not at the ranch, he'll either be at the bar or his apartment above it. I have no doubt I'll find him.

I just loaded my last box of jams into my truck bed and climbed into the driver's seat. The drive to town goes quickly, and I pull into the parking lot on the edge of Main Street.

There is parking in front of the shops, but if I tried to parallel park, I would owe a lot of people a lot of money. It is much safer for all parties if I park in the lot.

I've come prepared, don't worry. I brought a dolly and will load up my boxes, then push them the few blocks to the diner.

I don't even get funny looks anymore pulling a stack of jams behind me. Now, people just wave and kindly step out of my path.

As I approach the retro diner, a man I recognize as one of Emmett's rodeo friends holds the door open for me. "Thanks, Brandon." I offer him a soft smile, and he returns one in kind.

"Need help unloading those?" He asks and waves his hand at my boxes.

I'm more than capable of unloading them by myself, but I wouldn't mind having someone do it for me. "You don't mind?"

"For you," he smirks. "Not at all."

Okay, so he's flirting with me. Great. Nothing beats unsolicited advances.

He's started loading my boxes into the store room, so I go to the front counter and have the manager, Addy, sign for the delivery.

We talk for a few minutes about nothing in particular. I compliment her gorgeous dress, and she tells me I can borrow it anytime.

"Who's the cutie helping you with those boxes?" She wiggles her eyebrows.

I roll my eyes at the insinuation. "He's one of Emmett's rodeo buddies." I don't mention that I have no interest in any man besides Hudson.

"So, you don't mind if I take a shot at him?"

I giggle. She's the town bombshell and could have anyone she wanted. "I think that sounds like fun."

We both start laughing, but I startle when a large hand lands on my lower back. I'm wearing a short cut shirt today, so the fingers graze my bare flesh.

My skin breaks out in goose bumps, but not the kind that's good.

I turn around and see Brandon standing far too close to me. I try to step away, but he doesn't budge.

"All done, babe. Wanna grab a drink next door?"

I can't stop the laugh that jumps out of me. I have zero interest in spending time with any man who isn't Hudson. "Actually, my boyfriend owns the bar, so that might get a little awkward."

His hand is still touching me. "Well," he leans in even closer. "I don't see a boyfriend."

When he pulls back, he winks at me, and I all but gag. What a bold fucker. I open my mouth to tell him to get his nasty hands off of me when his body is abruptly pulled away from mine.

I feel a warm presence at my back, and a set of familiar arms wrap around my waist, pulling me flush against his body. I know immediately that it's Hudson. His smell, size, and gentleness give him away.

I lean further into him, and he presses a kiss to the top of my head.

"Now you see him," Hudson growls. "Touch her again and I'll break your arm."

I shouldn't like the violent possessiveness, but my insides warm at his declaration.

"Sorry, man." He says, raising his hands. "I would've stayed away if I had known."

"I heard her tell you she had a boyfriend. Is her word not as valuable as mine?" He cocks his head, his tone dangerous.

"No. No, it's not like that." He pleads.

"You're disgusting," he all but spits. "Don't show your face here again."

Brandon all but runs out of the diner, slamming the bell against the door as he goes.

I spin around in Hudson's arms and wrap mine around his back, feeling the thick muscles under my fingertips. Nuzzling my head deeper into his chest, he rests his lips on top of my head.

I pull back and look up at him. He looks miserable, wearing dark circles under his eyes and a thick layer of stubble. I feel emotion gathering behind my eyes.

"Hey, it's okay, ladybug," he coos and brushes my hair behind my ears.

"What are you doing here?" I have so many things I want to say to him, but they all blur as I stare into his bottomless brown eyes.

"I live next door," he teases.

I roll my eyes, and he leans close. His lips brush my forehead as he whispers, "I saw you from my window and couldn't stay away."

"I'm glad you didn't," I whisper back.

We will never stay away from each other again. No matter what happens, Hudson and I are a package deal.

Chapter Twenty-Four

Delilah

The Fortunate Fox is slammed tonight.

After Hudson publicly staked his claim to me, he practically carried me to his apartment, where we spent the entire day reacquainting our bodies.

My lips are swollen from his kisses, and my body tender from his touch. Yet, I would remain for the rest of my days if it meant I could feel his devotion the way I am now.

When the sun made its farewell, Hudson peeled us out of bed and cleaned us up in the shower. He massaged my scalp as he washed my hair and pressed soft kisses all over my body as he washed me. My body still hums from his lingering touch.

He went down to check on the bar and found the staff struggling to keep up with all the patrons.

He came back upstairs to tell me he needed to help them and made me promise I'd still be in his bed waiting for him when he was finished. I did him one better and went down to the bar with him.

I tried to help behind the counter, but I was just getting in everyone's way, so I sat on the stool at the far corner of the bar away from everyone. This seat does give me the perfect view of Hudson's muscles in that tight t-shirt he's wearing, which I'm very much enjoying.

I don't even try to hide my stares. There's no one else I want to look at, and he's just so handsome. Every once in a while, I see him scanning the crowd, but then stop when he finds me in the same seat. His smile is blinding every time he meets my eyes.

We haven't talked about the strain we've been experiencing, but he's acting completely normal, so I'm trying to savor it while I can.

I know we will eventually need to have that conversation, but for now, I'm happy to simply pretend there is no strife.

He's playing bartender and waiter tonight, so there have been periods where he disappears from view for a few minutes, but he always stops by my stool on his way back from the seating area and wraps his arms around me from behind, squeezing me tight. I can't help but giggle like a schoolgirl every time he does it. Being wrapped up in his arms feels so right, like I'm meant to be there.

He kisses a trail down my jaw and whispers in my ear, "I need to help in the kitchen for a while, will you be okay out here?"

He keeps pressing soft kisses to my neck, making my body buzz. "I'll be fine, but I don't want you to stop doing this."

His chuckle is low and deep, making goosebumps rise on my skin. "I know, ladybug. I want nothing more than to bury myself between your thighs right now, but I promise if you can be a good girl and wait a little longer, I'll spend the rest of the night making you come over and over. On my fingers, on my tongue, on my cock." Then pulls away, a few inches from my lips, and winks at me.

My core tingles at his promise, and my brain goes hazy thinking about him.

"You still with me?" He asks teasingly.

"I'm here, just *really* don't want you to go." I exaggerate my words, drawing them out for effect.

His lips quirk, bringing out his sexy dimples. "Every minute I'm away from you, I spend thinking about being with you."

If I weren't already positive I was in love with him, this would seal the deal.

He disappears into the kitchen, and I start wiping down beer glasses to help the staff.

The busy work keeps me distracted from the chaos all around me. Don't get me wrong, I enjoy a bit of fun on a night out, but I don't want any fun if Hudson's not standing beside me.

Above the bar are a few TVs playing various sports games, and I zone in on the one playing a hockey game. It's not the Windrunners, Henely's team, but I watch regardless.

I fall into a rhythm of wiping and washing, but a loud cheer from the pool tables breaks my flow.

The hooping and hollering feels a bit excessive, and I can't help but roll my eyes.

"Better luck next time, old man," I hear someone shout.

It's the deep, crackly voice I hear next that makes the hairs on the back of my neck stand on end. "Just you wait! My boy owns this bar, and he's the best player in the state!"

Peering over my shoulder, I see Hudson's dad pointing a finger at a younger man's chest.

It's been years since I last saw him, and time has not been kind to him. He's much more gaunt than I remember, and his hair is completely gray. There was a time when I saw the resemblance between him and his son, but now I couldn't find a similarity if I tried.

What is he doing here? Hudson told me he bought this place specifically so his dad wouldn't come here.

He's starting to make a scene at the tables. I can't hear exactly what they're saying, but I see it's getting heated.

Before I can stop myself, I'm all but running up to him.

When I step between him and the stranger he's fighting with, recognition dawns on him. His wrinkly old face cracks a smile, and he traps me in a bear hug. The smell of stale booze and cigarettes consumes me, and I try not to gag.

When I'm free from his hold, he says, "Look at Little Lilah, all grown up."

I'm not sure how to answer him, so I keep it casual. "How are you, Mr. Owens?"

He gives me a genuine smile, and for a moment, he looks sober. "I'd be a whole lot better if these jackholes would listen to me."

I need to cut to the chase. I won't converse with him in this state. "I don't want to sound rude, but I think you should leave."

The mask of happiness fades, his face transforming into one of rage. He steps toward me, but I step back. "Don't you go acting like you're better than me, girl. He's my boy, and nothing you say is going to change that," he all but spits at me.

Before I have a chance to fire a retort, something along the lines of *He's mine in ways you'll never understand*, Hudson's arm wraps around my waist and protectively pulls me behind him. "She said you should leave," he growls in a voice I don't recognize as my sweet Hudson's.

His dad looks at the way he's holding me and bursts out laughing. "Well, look at you. You finally got the girl, huh?" He's mocking Hudson, and I hate it.

"Stay away from her." In all my years of knowing Hudson, I have never heard him sound so angry.

"I have no interest in her. I just need you to play a few rounds for me and show these halfwits how pool is played."

Based on the stories Hudson told me, his dad has bet money on him winning.

"I don't do that anymore." I barely notice it, but I can hear a hint of shame in his voice. I squeeze my hand in his to let him know I support him, and he squeezes mine back.

His dad looks between us with a blank stare. "Just once for your old man, alright. Then you can go back to Lucky Liliah." He waves his hand dismissively at me.

"What did you call her?" His voice is low. Dangerous.

"She always brought me luck, ya know," he singsongs. I don't know what he's talking about. I only ever saw him briefly when he worked on the ranch.

He looks directly at Hudson now. "You wanted to stay at the ranch so bad. Wanted to be close to her. You knew winning would keep me put, so you made sure to win every game you played, and she's the reason why. So, she's always been my secret lucky charm."

The muscles in Hudson's arm tighten, and I'm worried he's going to punch his dad. I stroke my thumb over his veins a few times until I feel him relax.

How could a father use his child the way he did Hudson? Taking a desire for a home and twisting it into a manipulation tactic is disgusting and cruel. I'm about to tell him as much, but Hudson beats me to it. "You used me my entire life, you disgusting old man." Mr. Owens dares to look hurt, as if he doesn't treat his son like expendable dirt. "Don't you dare say that Del was your luck. She was the reason I got up every morning after being dragged to nameless bars every night by you. I was so desperate to see her that I would do anything, including being your worker boy. She is luck to me. Without her, I would have probably turned out exactly as you are now, set to die on a smoke-stained stool in the corner of some dive bar. I'm lucky I had her then, and I'm even luckier I have her now. Get the hell out of my bar and never come back."

I feel a warm tear gliding down my face, but I can't take my eyes off of Hudson. At some point during his speech, I stopped looking at his dad and got lost in the deep brown eyes that belong to Hudson.

A rough thumb wipes the tear away from my eyes. "Why are you crying, baby?" His voice is now so gentle, the complete opposite of the way he spoke to his father.

I don't answer, just collapse into his chest and let him hold me. And he does. He holds me in the bar where everyone can see. He holds me as he carries me to his apartment. He holds me as I fall asleep on top of him, not wanting any space between us.

After everything he's been through, he finally stood up to his dad. I am so proud of him. He deserves someone who cherishes him and loves him unconditionally. As I drift off to sleep, flat on his chest, I vow to be that person.

Chapter Twenty-Five

Hudson

Ever since the night at the bar a few days ago, I feel so light. Like a weight has been lifted off my shoulders.

I finally stood up to him. Oddly enough, having Del standing next to me made it possible.

I didn't like him calling her his luck. That's what made me snap. She's mine—every part of her.

She gave me the confidence I needed to finally tell him to get out of my life. Her gentle touch kept me grounded and focused.

My dad didn't look hurt, per se. More confused. As if he truly didn't think I could deny him a request.

I feel a sense of sadness. Not so much for my father, but more of what I hoped for. I always wanted him to love me and treat me like Mr. Walton did his kids. I knew deep down it would never happen, but having him out of my life completely is bringing everything into perspective.

It might sound wrong, but I'd choose Del over him any day. She has always been there for me. Even when she had no idea the impact she had on me. Her happiness always gave me the strength to keep moving forward.

I wasn't going to let him stand in *my* bar and disrespect *my* woman.

It was like something in me snapped. I didn't care if I ever saw him again as long as he got away from Del.

Adrenaline was surging through my veins, but her light touch across my arms and her soft voice telling me it was okay calmed me right down.

Crawling into bed that night with her little body wrapped around mine made everything I've ever been through feel worth it.

She fell asleep first, curled snuggly against me, while I ran my fingers through her hair as her warm breath fell over my bare chest.

I don't care what I have to do, but I will fix things with her brothers.

If they never want to speak to me again, I can live with that.

What I can't live with is spending a single day away from Del again.

Henley told me they would come to their senses, but I know them well enough to know that it won't be that simple.

Right now, I'm the villain.

If they come around, I will forgive them for the things they said about me. I will keep the peace so Del doesn't feel the burden. She will have her brothers and me, because I will not allow her to choose between us.

I can't live without her, and I will not make her live without her family.

I don't know how I can convince them that I will cherish her for the rest of my life, but I will find a way to do so.

I will make this right, so Del and I can be together. There is simply no other option. She is mine, and I am hers.

Chapter Twenty-Six

Hudson

Known by locals only, the town of Stone Lake actually has a lake named after it. Or, more likely, the town was named after the lake.

Our great secret. Hidden deep in the woods is a lake that has housed countless teenage parties, endless children's first swims, and an uncountable number of weekend camping trips. Which is precisely what Del and I are doing this weekend.

Being away from her for so long made me realize that I never want to be away from her again. I want to spend our days and nights together.

I decided I needed to make up for lost time. The few days I spent wallowing were wasted, and I intend to make up for it.

I told Del to pack a bag and tack up Izarra, then we met at the river and started riding to Stone Lake. The horses moved slowly, and for a while, we held hands as our horses carried us.

Everyone who grew up here knows the way. There are beaten-down paths you can follow, but if you aren't looking for them, you'll miss them.

I think the Walton boys and I have created our fair share of these paths ourselves. The thought of them ignites a twinge in my chest. I look over at Del and find her head tipped up towards the sun. Eyes closed, just letting the breeze dance across her skin, and the crack starts to patch.

A smile grows on my face as I watch her. She is so beautiful, not even the rays beating through the trees can compete.

"You're freaking me out," she says without so much as looking at me. She must be able to sense my eyes on her.

"Can't help myself, baby."

Her eyes meet mine, and she hits me with her sexy eyes. The look that makes my cock thicken painfully quickly. Definitely not a good idea while in the saddle, but I'm powerless against her.

I shift back and forth a few times before readjusting myself in my jeans.

"Something bothering you, big guy?" she taunts.

Damnit. She saw me. She already knows what she does to me. It's no secret.

"Yeah, ladybug, there is. You gave me those fuck me eyes while I'm trapped on this horse."

She giggles, so light and airy. The birds chirp in tandem with her, creating a beautiful, earthly melody.

"It's not my fault you have the control of a dolphin," she rolls her eyes at me.

"A dolphin?" I question.

Her attention shifts from the path ahead back to me. "Yeah, a dolphin." Her lids lower, and she bites her lip seductively. "I heard they're incredibly sexual creatures. They have sex for pleasure, not just conception. Sounds a lot like what I want you to do to me right now."

That little minx. I'm about thirty seconds from dismounting and taking her on the forest floor. "Watch it, Del, or you won't like what happens."

"Oh, I'm pretty sure I will."

Okay, that's it. I pull back my reins, and Lucky slows to a stop. Del keeps walking her horse forward, looking over her shoulder at me. "What are you doing back there? Just enjoying the view?" She asks while wiggling her butt in her saddle.

I must be losing it because I feel a sudden, violent rush. Towards her saddle. What is wrong with me? Oh, wait, I know. I'm desperately in love with her. And, apparently, jealous of a saddle.

"I am now," I say while unabashedly checking her out.

"Well, get used to the view from behind, because that's all you'll be seeing for the next little while." Then she winks at me, clicks her heels, and Izarra takes off running down the path.

When I catch her, get my hands on her, I'll remind her not to run away from me. If she runs, I'll catch her.

I dig my heels in and click at Lucky to take off after her.

She blurs through the pines as I chase the distance between us. Her coffee-brown hair sways freely as the breeze takes hold of it.

I hear her laughing at herself, which only spurs me on.

She's too far ahead of me to be able to see her now, but I can still make out the clomping noise of horse hooves on the forest floor.

Lucky's a bit wider than Iz, so we have to take the trail slower. I can't risk his stumbling on a root or scraping his sides.

I'll let her win this round. I know she'll bring it up for the rest of our lives, but it's a necessary loss.

When I finally reach the clearing by the lake, I find Iz tied to a branch near the water and Del sprawled out on a blanket she laid out on the sand.

The crystal water sparkles with patches of glitter as the sun rains down on its little waves. A curtain of tall pines serves as a backdrop, enveloping us in our private dome.

Even from the forest edge, past the soft white sand, I can see the stones decorating the bottom of the lake.

The lake's water is more transparent than glass. You can see the multicolored stones at the bottom from any depth. There is no muck, only rocks and stones. Hence, Stone Lake.

I swing my legs around the saddle and push myself away, landing on the ground with a thud, and start walking Lucky to a tree near Izarra.

"Took you long enough," Del chides. She pushes up to lean back on her elbows and swishes her hair over her slender shoulders.

I secure Lucky's reins to a branch and start walking over to her. "What can I say, I enjoy the view of you from behind too much."

"You're so bad," she teases and rolls onto her stomach.

"Baby, I can be a whole lot worse." Then I drop to my knees and use both hands to push her hair back. I keep the gathered piece in one of my fists and use the leverage to angle her head back. Her pulse thrums on her exposed neck, and I lean down to kiss it.

"Please," she moans. I groan and nibble her neck.

Her begging is the most beautiful thing I've ever heard.

"Not yet, baby." I have to set up our tent and get a fire going before we can have any real fun. I want to have both ready for her in case she gets tired or hungry.

Regretfully, I put some distance between us so I don't accidentally fuck her here and now. "Will you gather some sticks for the fire while I set up the tent?"

She pretends to think a bout it for a moment, quirking her mouth. "I could, but I think I'd much rather watch the show."

She pushes herself to standing, and I follow her lead. We both start our designated jobs, her finding branches and sticks and putting them in the premade fire pit, while I wrestle with the tent.

She finishes her job before I do, so she ultimately does end up getting a show. I hear her laughing at me as I curse under my breath.

"Hey, Hudson," she calls from a few feet away.

I brush the tent fabric away from my face and look over at her. "Everything okay, ladybug?"

"Yes, just checking in to see how everything's going?" She asks so sweetly that someone may think she's being genuine. But I know her well enough to know she's reveling in my struggle.

"Not great, baby."

She sticks out her bottom lip in a pout and cocks her head to the side, looking downright edible standing in front of me with that sexy little expression.

"Can I help? I think I know just what to do." The goddamn inventor of this thing wouldn't be able to help me, so I'm not sure what she's going to do.

Then she surprises me by pulling her t-shirt over her head, leaving her standing before me in nothing but a pair of tiny shorts.

Her nipples pinch at the fresh air. The rosy little buds reaching towards me. She looks otherworldly as the sun rains down on her.

I'm sitting here slack jawed with a tent wrapped around me and a raging boner in my pants when she takes it a step further and unbuttons her shorts and shimmies them down her legs, kicking them into a pile with her shirt.

Now, she's standing with only a pair of cotton panties in front of me, looking like every wet dream I've ever had come to life.

She brings her hands up to her neck and draws them down her chest, over her swollen nipples, and down her waist. I swear I come a little from her show.

Right as I start to stand up, she turns around and runs straight into the lake, fully submerging herself.

When her head pops back up, she's standing about waist-deep in the water; delicate water droplets glide down her exposed skin, tracing her soft curves.

My girl is perfect in every form, but seeing her naked and wet in front of me is almost too much to handle.

"Now you have an incentive. Once you've finished setting up the tent, you can join me. Until then..." She trails off and starts to float on her back.

As I stare at the water lapping around her bare skin, I hear her laughing at herself. My girl thinks she is so funny.

She may be a little trickster, but she has infallible logic because I find myself becoming the tent-building expert. Suddenly, the poles and holes all align perfectly, and the tent begins to take shape.

Before long, my shirt and jeans get discarded, and I'm in the water. It's too cold to be comfortable, and I don't want Del to stay in the water much longer. She likes to act tough, but it's my job to protect her. She'd never admit to having a limit, which means I need to dictate them for her.

I wrap my arms around her and cradle her to my chest. Her hands wrap around my neck, and her legs wrap around my waist. She grinds her pussy on my cock through our wet clothes. The damp fabric must cause a delicious friction on her clit because she moans and throws her head back.

I start walking us to the shore, but when she senses us moving, she pulls back with a confused expression on her face. "Where are you going?"

"I'm taking you to the tent."

She shakes her head back and forth. "Not yet," she says and circles her hips again. "I want you to fuck me in the water."

She is my strongest temptation. The urge to take her right now is almost overwhelming, but then I feel her shiver in my arms, and I focus.

I squeeze her body closer to mine, hoping she can get some of my body heat. "No, ladybug. You're too cold. Let me get you warmed up, and then I'll do whatever you want."

"I'm not that cold, Hudson." She says while goose bumps decorate her skin and her teeth chatter.

I ignore her and carry her to land, setting her down by the fire and wrapping a blanket around her shoulders, before I grab one for myself and snuggle in next to her.

Once we both have a chance to warm up, I throw on a pair of sweats and pull one of my shirts over her head. She looks so good in my clothes. Like she belongs in them.

I cook us some camp food and we eat as the stars come out to decorate the sky.

Before migrating into the tent for the night, we check on our horses, giving them fresh food and water.

Once we climb into the tent, she reaches behind her back and braids her hair into a beautiful rope, before she reaches under my shirt she's wearing and pulls down her panties.

The knowledge that she's wearing nothing besides my shirt does things to my brain. Things that involve her in my arms while my cock thrusts inside her.

After her swim in the lake, she came in here and made a bed for us. Instead of two separate sleeping bags, she unzipped them both to make two big blankets for us. I like that she doesn't want to be separated from me.

She crawls under the cover and holds her hand out to me. "Come to bed."

Obediently, I crawl under the cover and snuggle up to her, pulling her body on top of mine.

Her skin is warm from the fire outside, feeling like a blanket of its own.

"Thank you for bringing me here," she whispers as she nuzzles her cheek into my chest.

"I never want to be away from you again. I'm sorry I disappeared." I shouldn't have secluded myself from her. I was feeling hurt, but I'm sure she was too. It was selfish of me to leave her to deal with that on her own.

She's quiet for a moment, her heart beating in a steady rhythm. "You're here now," she whispers.

I shift our bodies so she's lying underneath me. I keep one hand cradled on the back of her skull so it doesn't touch the rough ground, and nudge her knees apart until I can settle my hips between hers. I lower myself to my forearms so our faces are only inches apart.

"I will never leave you again. Not for a single day."

Her ocean eyes widen, and a splash of fear shoots into my chest. Did I freak her out?

She wets her bottom lip with the tip of her tongue, and her eyelashes flutter.

Her soft breath hits my face, and goosebumps erupt on my exposed arms and chest.

I need her to say something.

Her soft hands land on my shoulders, my muscles flexing in response.

"Promise?" She whispers, her eyes hazy with desire.

Now it's my turn to look surprised.

She wants me. Me.

Regardless of the struggles with her family, we are going to face, and despite my upbringing, which still floods into my life. She chooses me.

"As long as you want me." I feel strangely exposed saying it. I want her more than I want the sun to rise tomorrow. She could toss me aside, and I would still love her.

Her hands move to cup my cheeks, the soft skin of her hands rubbing against my stubble. "I have wanted you from the moment we met all those years ago. I would have wanted you for the rest of my life even if we hadn't gotten together. Now that I have you, I never want to lose you. I want to spend every day for the rest of my life with you. Regardless of the problems with our families, Hudson. I don't care. As long as we have each other, we will be okay. I know everything will be okay with my brothers and your dad as long as I have you."

God, this woman is perfect for me, and I will spend every day for the rest of my life earning her.

Her eyes flash to my lips, silently begging me to seal our mouths together.

So I do.

I kiss her softly and deeply until my lips start to tingle. My tongue separates her swollen lips, and she lets me in; our tongues collide in a sensual dance, fusing us together.

Her thighs tighten around my hips as she grinds her bare pussy against my throbbing cock. I let her tease us both while I grab a condom out of my bag and roll it on.

I rub the tip of my cock through her dripping fold, groaning as I feel her wetness coat me.

Each time I graze her clit she whimpers, making me impossibly harder. But I don't stop. I keep rubbing myself on her while we kiss.

She pulls away first, leaving us both gasping for air. "Please," she whines, digging her nails into my back. The sting feels so good. Almost as good as her desperation feels. "I can't take it anymore. Fuck me."

I did say I'd give my girl anything she wants.

I guide myself into her dripping entrance and slowly thrust in. She's so tight around my shaft that I can't help but moan into her soft neck.

The walls of her pussy throb around me making tingles dance up my spine.

I fuck her slowly, moving my hips in and out at a languid pace, drawing out our pleasure. I keep her wrapped safely in my arms, pressing light kisses to her neck, her lips, her face.

She moans so sweetly as I tease the delicate spot deep inside her.

A red blush appears on the apples of her cheeks, a telltale sign of her impending orgasm. I grab her hips and angle them so I can reach even deeper inside her.

She locks her arms around my neck and guides my lips back to hers.

We kiss slowly, my hips pumping steadily and deeply inside her. She starts to tremble. Her body so small under mine, beginning to crumble from her pleasure.

I swallow her gasps as she shatters, he pussy squeezing me so tight I have no choice but to follow her. We come together, using each other's breath as air. Her most delicate muscles tremble around me, and I feel my vision go hazy.

I have never come so hard in my entire life. Every time we fuck, the pleasure reaches a new level. But this felt different. I would never consider what Del and I do just to be *fucking*. She matters too much to me for that. Each time our bodies join, our souls do too.

This time, we used our bodies to convey to each other what we're too afraid to say with our words. My body told her I love her enough to stand up to my father and her brothers, anything that stands in our way. Her body told me the same, that she loves me enough to fight for us.

We keep kissing long after we come down from our orgasm high. Once both of our heartbeats slow, I lay down beside her, allowing her to swing her leg and arm across me. She rests her head in the crook of my shoulder, and I brush my fingers down her spine until her body relaxes and she falls asleep.

Nuzzling my nose into her hair, I take a long smell of her fruity scent and immediately feel my eyes flutter closed. She makes me feel relaxed. Safe. She cares for me just the way I am and wants nothing from me besides my love.

I will spend the rest of my life giving it to her.

She's deep asleep, her soft snoring filling the tent. Even though she can't hear me, I press a lingering kiss to her forehead before whispering, "I love you, Delilah Walton."

I swear she blushes, but it must be my mind playing tricks on me.

Soon. I'll tell her I love her soon.

Once I fix things with her family.

I need to fix this for her. I know better than to tell her not to worry. She thinks it's her responsibility to keep the peace between us all, but it's not. It's me that they're upset with. Not her.

We're both stressed over them, the tension looming in the air, but neither of us is willing to give the other up to make them happy.

This weekend is for us. A chance for me to make up for my absence from her. But once we get home, I'll start working on mending things with her family. Even if they keep hating me, I will deal with it for her.

I will do everything possible to make the situation as peaceful as possible for her. The goal is to make her think everything is back to the way it was before. Deep down, I don't believe that's truly possible, but for her, I will make it happen.

Chapter Twenty-Seven

Delilah

I heard him.

Last night, after I *fell asleep.*

I wasn't actually sleeping, just basking in his adoration. He kept stroking my hair and touching my back. He kept kissing my face and tightening his grip on me.

I have never felt so adored.

I swear, my heart flooded with love from feeling how tender he was with me. His gentleness with me showed me how deep his feelings for me actually are.

And then, so quietly that I almost missed it, he told me he loves me.

My heart stopped beating, and I struggled not to react. Not because I was upset that he said it. The complete opposite, actually.

Clearly, he wasn't ready to tell me if he waited until I was asleep to do it. He was probably afraid I wouldn't say it back.

I've never told someone I love them before. I've never wanted to, but every time I think of Hudson's smiling face and the way he cradles me in his arms, I do.

I want him to know that I love him. That I want him despite my brother's disapproval.

He brings me peace and happiness, which is all my brothers have ever wanted for me.

The longer I've had to think, the more confident I am that they will come to see how beneficial this relationship is for all of us.

What I'm worried about is Hudson's friendship with them. They said things to him with the intention of hurting him. I don't know how they will make it up to him, but they better figure something out.

Whether they like it or not, Hudson will always be a part of my life. And so will they. I'm not giving up any of them, so they will need to find a way to work their shit out.

The faint smell of smoke from last night's fire permeates the air, making my nose twitch. I stretch my aching limbs, sore from sex and sleeping on the ground, before I sit up. The sleeping bag slips down my body, exposing my bare chest to the chilly morning air.

I dig through Hudson's bag until I find one of his long-sleeved shirts and slip it over my head. When I stand up, it hits me mid-thigh, covering most of my body.

The zipper pulls down on the tent, and the door falls away to reveal Hudson sitting on a log beside the fire. He looks so handsome in the early morning light, his hair tousled and his eyes a little puffy.

He looks over his shoulder when he hears me and gives me a childlike smile. I love that, after all these years, he still looks at me the same way. I never thought he loved me the way I did, but now that I see how he looks when he's in love, I realize he has always felt this way.

"Good morning, my beautiful girl."

I smile so hard it hurts. Yeah, I could get used to waking up with him.

When I get close enough to him, I wrap my arms around his neck from behind and press a few kisses on his cheek. "Good morning, my handsome man."

A groan rumbles in his chest before he pulls my mouth to his, kissing me deeply.

Yes, this is definitely a good morning.

He pulls back, licking his lips. "Mhhh," he groans. "I love the way that sounds."

"What? Me calling you handsome?"

"I like that, but I love you calling me your man," he says and gives me another deep kiss.

"You are, aren't you?" We've never had a conversation about our *status*. He feels like mine, and I want to be his.

"Ladybug, I have always been your man."

A sense of security fills me from the inside out. He's mine. "Does that make me your girlfriend?"

He rolls his eyes at me but keeps a loose hold on my nape. "The term doesn't feel strong enough for what you are to me, but it's a good place to start."

He leaves me speechless. He's right. The term doesn't feel strong enough. We feel connected in a way that wouldn't make sense to anyone who hasn't experienced it.

"Titles can change, but the way I feel about you won't," I whisper. Suddenly, I feel a bit vulnerable.

As if he can sense the shift, he burrows his head into my stomach and bands his arms around my middle. "I've known you were the other half of my soul from the first day I saw you. It might sound silly, but something clicked that day. Something that cemented you as the other half of my soul. I feel lucky that I've got to spend so much of my life with you, even if I had to love you from afar."

He says all this with his head hiding in my shirt. Probably for the best since I feel a tear glide down my cheek. I wipe it away before twining my fingers through his soft strands.

"I love you, Hudson," I whisper down at him.

I was going to wait. Tell him once I fixed everything, but I want him to know.

His head snaps up, his chin resting on my stomach as he gazes up at me with a pair of puppy dog eyes. From an outside perspective, he is a big, strong rancher. But the people who know him closest know that he's a big softy. Big and strong, yes, but always in tune with his softer side. It's something I've always appreciated about him.

"You love me?" I hear a hint of desperation in his tone, as if he needs my words to be true.

I run my fingers through his hair. His lashes lower. "I love you like the way clovers love the earth. They need it to survive."

His fingers dig into my flesh, so tightly it feels like he's worried I'll slip away. He clears his throat, his eyes taking on a glassy hue. His voice cracks when he speaks, "I love you with everything I have. Everything that I am."

A tension releases from around us. Like a collective weight has been lifted off of us since we both admitted our feelings.

I drop onto his lap and kiss him. Slow and deep. Our tongues collide as we touch every part of each other's bodies that we can reach.

He pulls away when a burning smell hits the air. "Shit," he grumbles and sets my body on the spot next to him.

Using a loose stick, he pulls a tinfoil packet out of the smoldering flames.

He uncrumples the silver foil and reveals a clump of burnt food.

Waving my hand in front of my face to get the smell away, I ask, "What is that?" It doesn't smell like anything besides singe.

Hudson sighs in disappointment. "I was trying to make you breakfast in bed. These were supposed to be potatoes."

Using all my willpower, I fight a laugh. He is such a sweet man, and he looks genuinely distraught over messing up.

We were planning on heading back later today, so we didn't pack much food, but I did sneak a few red apples into my bag. They were supposed to be treats for Iz and Lucky, but I don't think they'll mind sharing.

Hudson watches me push off my seat and walk over to my bag. I bend at the waist and reach into my backpack to find the apples. The farther I bend, the more Hudson oversized shirt rides up and before I know it, cool air hits my bare pussy.

I forgot I wasn't wearing panties.

The heat of Hudson's gaze bores into the back of me, setting me on fire.

"Fuck," he groans under his breath.

I try to right myself and use my hands to pull the shirt to cover myself. He's already seen every intimate part of me, but I can't help the instinct to shield myself.

Something rustles behind me before his hands meet my waist, and his face is buried into my neck. His breath warms my skin, and his prickly stubble activates my sensitive nerves.

"What are you doing to me?" His voice is low and pained.

I try to spin to face him, but he keeps my back pressed to his front. "Oh, I was grabbing something for us to eat."

He drags his nose up my neck before settling his mouth over my ear. "Del, you just offered me the best meal I'll ever eat."

What is he talking about?

Oh, wow.

My cheeks heat as I feel him drop to his knees behind me. The calluses on his hands scrape my soft flesh as he drags them up the back of my thighs, collecting the long shirt and pushing it to gather at my waist.

I'm completely exposed. Bent over with my most sensitive area on full display to him.

I try to stand up, but he puts a reassuring hand on my lower back, stilling my movements. His touch is grounding, and I immediately feel at ease.

"Stay still, love. I want to eat my breakfast." Then his tongue is lapping at my pussy like he's starving. Tongue, teeth, and lips work me until I'm a pool of pleasure in his arms.

This time, when I crumble, it's as if my world has spun out of control. Every orgasm Hudson gives me is more intense than the last, but this one feels different.

This time, I don't just feel his love, but have his words ringing in my head.

I thought I would spend my life loving him quietly. Now that he knows I love him and he loves me back, I want everyone to know. I want to walk hand in hand and let the entire town know he's mine.

I will not let anyone, not even my brothers, take this away from me.

I'm choosing to believe that once the initial shock of our relationship wears off, they will see how happy we are and give us their *blessing*.

Not that I need permission to be with him, because I don't. I really just want them to make things right with Hudson.

He's telling me he's fine, but I know he's hurting, and that pisses me off the most. My man is hurt, and it's my idiot brothers' fault.

I shake my head to clear my thoughts. This is a problem for when we get home. Right now, I'm going to sit curled up in my boyfriend's arms and watch the sun rise.

Chapter Twenty-Eight

Delilah

Admittedly, I have not been very eager to leave Hudson's vicinity. He's so warm and loving.

Finally being able to love him the way I want to is freeing. He's always been my best friend, and that hasn't changed. It amazes me how I can tell him he resembles the frying pan after I scramble eggs, and he answers by saying *At least I don't smell like the bottom of a cowboy boot,* and then we end up making out.

It is everything I've ever wanted. Him just the way he is. Only now I can touch him.

And let's just say, all the fantasies I've ever had about him don't compare to the real thing. They never accounted for the spark of electricity that zaps my skin or the flutter of my heart when he touches me back.

They definitely didn't consider the overwhelming feeling of contentment that washes over me whenever we're together. And I don't just mean sex. That's an out-of-body experience in itself, but just being near him is enough.

We decided to go out to breakfast this morning to the local hotspot, our only restaurant open before four p.m., the Dinky Diner.

The retro diner feels like a step back into the fifties, with blue leather seats and chrome countertops. There's a juke box in the corner and some neon lights around the trim. It's had the same menu since I was a child, and probably the same since my parents' childhoods.

They used to pile all of the kids, including Hudson, into the back of their pickup and drive us here for special occasions. Birthdays, rodeo wins, and good grades. No matter how menial it was, if it was important to any of us, they made sure we celebrated.

I have so many happy memories here with my family.

For a moment, I feel a sense of longing. I miss my parents. It's been a long time since we lost them, but the feeling of sadness never goes away.

Being estranged from my brothers doesn't help either.

Hudson rubs his hand absentmindedly across my thigh as we sit at the bar top. I look over at him, long strands of rich brown hair resting on his forehead. He's studying the menu with precision, as if it might have changed in the last fifty years.

I miss making memories with my family, but looking at the man sitting next to me, I feel a sense of calm. I will make new memories with the family we build. Even if it's just the two of us.

"What can I get for the cutest couple in town?" Addy, the waitress, asks. We went to high school together, but she was a few years older than me. Always wearing the most fabulous clothes and having to most friends, but besides that, she's nice to everyone. It's impossible not to like her. I'm pretty sure she even has Beckett on her good side, and not many people can say that.

She's also arguably the most beautiful woman in this entire town. Hudson looks up at her and answers, "I'll take the ranchman's special and my girl will get the party pancakes a la mode." Then he looks at me, and his eyes go from normal to swimming with affection. I feel myself fall into his love-filled look.

He doesn't even notice the beautiful woman in front of him. He only has eyes for me, and my heart thumps in response.

"You two are disgustingly perfect, and I love it." I don't want to be rude, so I begrudgingly pull my gaze from Hudson and face her.

She's staring at us with longing, almost looking a little sad. "You okay, Addy?"

She sighs, but flips her striking auburn hair over her shoulder and schools her features. If I didn't see the way her eyes glossed over, I wouldn't think anything was amiss. But I know that look. It's the look of wanting something that you can't have. I walked around with that look for a long time before I admitted my feelings for Hudson.

"Right as rain, Del." She shoots me with a flirty wink.

"Don't do that," Hudson says.

I look at him quizzically.

Addy giggles, but covers her mouth with her hand to try to block it. His eyes narrow at her in warning.

"Do what?" She asks.

The grip on my thigh tightens to a near-painful level. What is going on? Why is he going all possessive caveman on me?

"Wink at her." My fun, easygoing Hudson has left the building and has been replaced by a version of himself I've seldom seen before. His eyebrows are pulled together, and his forever smile has disappeared.

Both Addy and I start laughing, but Hudson doesn't join. He scowls at us both, and I feel tears pool in the corner of my eyes.

Addy throws her bracelet-covered hands into the air in mock surrender. "I'm no threat to you, Hudson," she says with an eyeroll. "Besides, someone who looks at you the way *she* looks at you is not looking anywhere else."

He keeps his gaze trained on his menu, but I swear the tips of his ears have gone red.

Before turning to head back in the kitchen, Addy looks at me and whispers, "I'm so happy you finally figured your shit out."

If Hudson hears, he doesn't say anything. In fact, he still has his head buried in the menu. Which is useless, considering we've already placed the order.

"Why are you hiding?" I poke him in the rib and he jumps, putting down his menu and facing me.

"I'm not hiding," he says, but his tone lacks conviction.

I shouldn't tease him.

Oh, that's ridiculous.

I'm gonna tease him *and* enjoy it.

"You wouldn't happen to be jealous, would you?"

He cocks his head to the side, looking deep into my eyes like he's searching for something. "So, what if I am?"

Oh my god. He is jealous.

I know I shouldn't love that he's jealous, but I really, really do.

"It was just Addy," I try to ease his mind. Even though I like his jealousy, I don't want him to worry.

"Yeah, but everyone likes Addy."

Is he serious? "Everyone likes you, too." I try not to sound bitter when I say it, but there is definitely a slight edge to my voice.

"I think your judgment is biased," he teases, and the tension from my emotions eases.

It's not that I'm self-conscious or anything. I'm just aware that Addy and I look different. I love the way I look and am proud to see myself in the mirror. I'm just conscious of the fact that Addy is super model gorgeous, while I'm girl-next-door cute. Both are perfect.

I just can't fight the self-deprecating thoughts in my head that Hudson would look better with her on his arm. He is arguably the most handsome man in Stone Lake.

The thought of anyone besides me on his arm sends a wave of nausea through me that makes my stomach knot.

"Hey, hey, ladybug. Where'd your head just take you?" His voice is so soft, and he leans in close, creating our own little space, secluding us from the world around us.

"Nowhere," I say, but when he lifts a questioning eyebrow, I say, "It's silly."

When I drop my gaze from his, he puts two fingers under my chin and lifts my face back to his.

Deep pools of affection stare at me, and I feel safe sharing my most inner thoughts. "I was just thinking how someone as handsome as you would look with someone as beautiful as Addy."

My words sound like whispers with how low I speak. I don't want the idea to get into his head and for him to realize it's accurate.

But that doesn't happen.

Despite being in a restaurant, he slams his lips to mine. He's not soft or slow. This kiss is a message. A message that I belong to him and he belongs to me.

When he pulls back, his eyes are dark with lust.

"I love you, Delilah Walton," he says in a firm tone. "I want to spend the rest of my life with *you* on my arm. I want to show *you* off and rub it in everyone's faces that you're mine. I don't want anyone else. I have never wanted anyone else. Only you." He whispers the last word like it's a plea.

I'm left speechless.

Hearing him say everything I've ever wanted to hear makes my brain stutter.

Too much time must pass of me staring open-mouthed at him because he speaks again. "Shit," he grumbles, raking a hand through his hair. "I shouldn't have said all that. I probably just freaked you out and ruined everything."

"No!" I all but scream at him.

God, I need to get a grip.

I just can't have him thinking I didn't love every word that just came out of his mouth.

He looks startled. Probably because I just yelled in his face.

I take a deep breath to settle my thoughts before looking him in the eyes, trying to convey all my love to him. "Say it again," I plead.

"Say what?"

"Tell me you love me, tell me you only want me. Please?"

His eyes soften. "I love you more than I even knew was capable. You're the luckiest thing that's ever happened to me, Del." He cups my jaw tenderly and rests his forehead against mine. "One day, I will marry you. Just like I told myself I would all those years ago when we stood in the back field looking for a four-leaf clover."

A tear falls down my cheek, but he's quick to wipe it away with his thumb. A watery *I love you* falls from my lips.

He stares at me with reverence as I wipe my eyes. "You know," I start. "The clover hanging in your truck is the first and only clover I've ever found."

His eyes widen with pure disbelief. "What?"

A chuckle falls from my lips. "Yeah, I found it before you took your driving test, and I wanted you to have the luck. You said you were nervous for it."

"Delilah," he says, but it sounds pained. "Why did you give me that? We spent forever trying to find one for *you*."

I'm not sure if I ever wanted a four-leaf clover for myself or if I just enjoyed spending time with him. We would spend hours in the fields together looking.

"I wanted you to have it. Maybe, I wanted you to think of me every time you saw it."

Now it's his turn to laugh at me. "Oh baby, I don't need a four-leaf clover to think about you."

I'm smiling so hard it hurts.

"You know," he starts in a singsong voice. "I found a four-leaf clover once?"

Well, this is new to me.

"And you never told me?" I feign shock, but I'm not sure how much faking I'm doing. I feel a little left out that he never told me.

"Yeah. The love of my life took her shirt off and there was one right next to her perfect tits."

I give him a playful smack on his bicep. "You're so bad," I admonish, but I can't stop the smile stretching across my face.

He winks at me just as an array of plates is set down in front of us. "Okay," a winded Addy says, wiping her perfectly manicured brow. "I waited as long as I could. You two are adorable, but I'm not going to hold these plates all day while you have some enviable moment."

"Sorry, Addy," I say sheepishly.

Her manicured hand waves through the air. "Don't sweat it, just enjoy it."

I plan to.

Every day for the rest of my life.

I turn to smile at Hudson, but he's already shoveling down his spread of food.

Feeling happier than I ever have, I focus on the food Hudson ordered for me. A plate of Funfetti pancakes and a bowl of ice cream.

I love him so much, and it's obvious he loves me too.

Chapter Twenty-Nine

Hudson

"Okay, so this is what I think we need to do..."

Delilah has sat me down for a pre-meeting.

We are planning to go talk to her brothers, but she wants us to have a plan in place. She says going in there guns a blazing is not a *real plan*.

Honestly, I have no thoughts in my head except *fix it*.

I miss my best friends.

I'm worried Del misses her brothers.

I feel like it's my fault.

All I know is I need Del and would really like my friends back.

As much as I've been enjoying all this quality time with my girl, I've been longing to see my friends.

Even though the question of our friendship is up in the air at the moment, I know I want them back.

After stepping back for a few weeks, I understand that they were in the heat of the moment. Del and Henely have also assured me that they didn't mean a word they said.

I'm not so sure about that.

If they said it, they must have meant it.

So, I'm stuck at a crossroads.

Forgive them or don't.

It would be better to push their words under the rug, but I'm not sure if we can go back to the way things were. Assuming, of course, that they would want that.

All I know is that I miss how things used to be.

If I got them back and had Del in my life, I would have everything I've ever wanted.

Could I be so lucky?

Part of me thinks anything is possible as I watch Del pace her kitchen in one of my shirts.

I should be paying attention to her. She's probably got everything she wants to say planned out, and she probably has lines I'm meant to memorize.

But I can't.

Her tan legs are on full display beneath *my* shirt. Her hair is tousled, and her cheeks are still flushed from all the orgasms I gave her before we got out of bed.

She has a big jam order going out at the end of the week, so she wanted to get some canning done this morning.

The house is already stifling from the stove being on for so long, so I'm sitting at the kitchen table in just a pair of sweatpants.

I've been tasked with placing her labels on top of the sealed jars once they've cooled. Luckily for me, it's not a very demanding job, so I get to watch her skillfully work while I munch on a bowl of fruit she set out for me.

If I could do this every day, I would. Wake up next to her, spend the day helping her with anything she was working on, then end the evening together in bed.

Even the boring, slow-moving days are enjoyable when she's around.

"Hudson, are you listening to me?" She asks while topping off my bowl of blueberries.

Running my fingers through my sleep-mussed hair, I answer. "Probably not as much as I should be," I admit.

She groans and pulls out a chair next to me and sits down. Too far away if you ask me, so I slide her chair closer to me until her legs are brushing mine. Much better.

"Hudson, this is serious," she admonishes and brushes my hand off her leg.

Unacceptable. I put it back.

Now that I'm allowed to touch her, I'm never going to stop.

She doesn't try to push me off this time, just rolls her eyes. I'm okay with that.

"We need to have a clear idea of what we want to say when we see them tonight."

I know she's right. Of course, she's right. If there's ever a question of who's right between the two of us, the answer is and always will be her.

"What do you want to say?" That's really the most important thing. Making sure she expresses herself. I'll back her up anyway she decides to go.

In this situation, I'd much prefer to be her sidekick slash bodyguard.

Is it cowardly? Potentially, but I feel so vulnerable.

They made me feel like a kid again. The same kid who wore sneakers that were too small and shirts that were too big. They made me feel small, despite knowing how hard I had worked to build myself up.

Like when a friendly dog suddenly bites for no reason. That's how their words made me feel.

That's why I'm not offering any suggestions to Del. Part of me just wants to hide behind her and let her say her peace.

The other part of me wants to call them out on their cruelty.

"Hudson?"

Shit. I can't keep my head straight.

"I'm sorry. I'm all ears."

Her eyes soften with sympathy, almost as if she knows exactly what's running through my head. "It'll all be okay," she promises.

I'm not so sure it will be, but I fake a smile and nod. "I know, love."

She seems pleased with my answer, so she continues telling me her plan and strategy. Everything she's saying makes sense; be direct, don't back down, stay assertive and confident.

I can do it.

I'll let Del take the lead and pick up from there.

After she makes me repeat the plan back to her, she climbs on my lap and lets me feed her the remaining berries from the bowl.

As I look down at her curled up in my lap, I feel a sense of determination wash through me.

For her, I will be brave.

For her, I will confront my biggest insecurity.

I will do anything she asks of me. Talking to her brother and my best friends is something I can handle.

The delicate rise and fall of her chest against mine solidifies my decision.

We will walk in together *and* walk out together. We will fix this together.

Chapter Thirty

Hudson

I'm quiet on the drive to the family farm, spending most of my time gazing at the setting sun out the windshield, taking notice of the golden hayfields. Stone Lake is arguably one of the most beautiful places in the world. I may be biased because I consider this place to be my home and saving grace, but my opinion is the only one that matters in this situation.

I have Del's hand clasped in mine, rubbing slow circles over her knuckles with my thumb. The motion is calming me as we get closer and closer.

We drove my truck, the same one I've had since I was sixteen years old. I have a flag pinned up on the roof and the four-leaf clover Del gave me hanging from the rearview mirror.

Just looking at it reminds me of the reason I'm doing this.

She loves me. She's always loved me, and I need to make things right for her.

My foot eases on the brake as we pull up to the familiar white farmhouse. There's no one on the wraparound front porch, but the storm door is propped open with a watering can, letting the breeze stream through the screen door.

We crank our windows closed, but neither of us makes a move to get out of the truck. There's an unspoken tension in the air. Both of us know the chances of this meeting going smoothly are slim to none, yet neither of us will say it out loud.

Trying to ease the tension in my chest, I take a slow, deep breath in through my nose and out through my mouth. After a few goes, I give up, realizing it's not working. I need something stronger. Shit, do I have a beer in the back?

No, I don't, but I think I know what will work better.

Sliding my hand across the worn knit seat, I reach my hand out to Del. She twines her fingers through mine, letting her warm, soft skin soothe me.

Her tiny hand squeezes mine once before she looks in my direction. Crystal blue eyes connect with mine, and I feel my expression soften. "It'll be okay," I tell her, even though I'm not sure I believe it.

She gives me a soft, halfhearted smile. "Either way, you and I are walking out of there together. Promise?"

That's the only thing I'm sure about this evening. "I promise."

"Alright then," she says and opens her truck door, pushing herself out and onto the gravel driveway. If we were to rank our collective comfort with this situation, hers would be higher than mine. Although this is awkward for both of us, they are her family and will accept her regardless. She will always have a place in their home. I, on the other hand, am an outsider. As much as I like to think I'm part of the family, in this situation, I'm the bad guy who defiled their baby sister.

Nevertheless, I follow her lead and do the same, jumping out of the truck and closing the door behind me. I walk around the front of my silver truck until I'm standing in front of her.

She has to tilt her head to look at me, but when our eyes meet, I see a hint of fear in them.

That is unacceptable.

I was nervous but now I'm pissed. How dare they make her feel this way? I won't let it stand.

My chest puffs out like I'm preparing for battle, and I start walking to the house, leaving Del standing in the driveway.

Suddenly, all my fear is gone, replaced with an overwhelming determination.

I swing the screen door open so hard it hits the side of the house, and I wince, but I don't stop. If I broke something, I'll fix it later.

I stomp my feet down the hardwood hallway until I round the corner and stop in the kitchen, where Cash, Emmett, and Beck are sitting around the breakfast table.

They're all wearing solemn expressions. Even Connie looks miserable. Her ears seem even droopier than usual. Not one howl or anything.

But I can't bother myself with asking what's going on; I need to get this out of my mind. "What the hell is wrong with all of you?" I ask bluntly.

Beckett's eyebrows rise to his hairline. I haven't seen him react so strongly to anything in years. Although he doesn't say anything, his eyes shine with what looks like pride.

Cash and Emmett take on sheepish expressions but remain silent.

"I'm seriously asking. I understand that you hate me, but making Del uncomfortable to come to her own farm is unacceptable!"

Padding feet that are unmistakably my Dels pad up behind me. She's breathing heavily, almost as if she ran to catch up with me. She stands next to me and gives me a *What the hell are you doing?* look.

Shit, I forgot about the plan.

"Sorry, ladybug," I whisper for her ears only.

She ignores me and steps in front of me to face her brothers. She's too cute for words, taking on a protective position in front of me. If we were in a different situation, I might find it amusing to see her little body acting like a protector. Though the idea that she *wants* to protect me only makes me love her more.

Letting her keep her superior position, I stand behind her in support.

I watch as her shoulders rise and fall as she takes a deep breath to steady herself. "Hudson and I would like to discuss our relationship with you all." She's so stoic, and her brothers seem much more receptive to her than to my sharp words.

"Alright," Beck says. I pull a chair out for Del and take the seat next to her, ensuring she's within arm's reach at all times. I don't know how this is going to go, and I want to be able to touch her if I need to. I want to feel close to her.

"Hudson and I are together." She says matter-of-factly, and I want to kiss her. She isn't ashamed of me.

"Whether you like it or not," I add, earning myself an icy glare from Del. I may be taking her carefully laid plan and lighting it on fire, but it feels good to get this off my chest.

Beckett surprises me by taking a hot dog off the center platter, throwing it on a bun, and taking a huge bite. He chews for a few beats as we all stare at him. Then, he calmly but surely says, "I like it."

What? Did I hear him right? He just said he likes that Del and I are together.

"Why are you making that face?" He asks.

I'm making this face because I don't understand. "I... well, I guess I'm a bit confused."

"Close your mouth, Hudson, or a bug will fly right in." I snap my mouth closed and shoot a glare at Cash. He's looking at me strangely. As if he's not sure what to say to me.

"Don't be a dick," Del snaps at him.

A red hue appears on his cheeks, sufficiently chastised by his sister. "Im not trying to be a dick I just... well I..." His words trail off, and he looks at Emmett for help.

Surprisingly, Emmett looks a bit embarrassed as well. His gaze is downcast, and I see him picking at the corner of his thumb.

"We all agree that you two make a fine couple," Beck says.

Del turns so fast in his direction that her fruity-smelling hair hits me across the face. "Excuse me?"

"You heard me," he says. "It's no surprise that you have feelings for each other. We have known it for years," he says and looks pointedly between the two of us. I thought I had done a pretty good job of hiding my feelings, but I guess I was wrong. "You have always had a soft spot for her, and we know that you will take care of her better than anyone else ever will."

"I will," I confirm without hesitation.

Cash is nodding along with Beck's words, but Emmett is still holding out, staring at me with a stony expression. "Is this what you think? Both of you?" I ask them both.

Cash runs a hand through his hair but speaks to Del when he answers. "If this is what you want, I will support you. He's a good man who will treat you right."

Her eyes soften as she smiles at him. "Thank you, Cashton."

Okay, three of her brothers have given their approval. I'm feeling good that this is going in the right direction. As long as I can get everyone to see that Del and I are not giving up on each other, it will be okay. I will learn to forget the things they said about me if it means Del is comfortable.

"And, Hudson? I'm sorry for punching you."

I can't help but laugh at him. It's not the first or the last time he'll throw a punch at me, but he sounds genuinely embarrassed for having done it. "Not cool, man," I jest.

"Oh, come on. I walk in on you and my baby sister. What did you think was going to happen?" He throws his hands up. The majority of the table falls into comfortable laughter. All of us except Emmett.

"Just say it, Em. Quite staring at him like he peed in your pudding and just spit it out!" This comes from my lovely little ladybug.

The muscle in his jaw twitches as he grinds his teeth together. "Really? It had to be Lilah?"

Okay, so he's definitely pissed and definitely doesn't want this relationship to happen. I just hope he doesn't bring up the cruel truths of my life like he did before. I don't know if I'll be able to handle it if he confirms that he really thinks so lowly of me.

"I love her, Emmett. I've always loved her, and I will *always* love her."

The silence in the room is deafening. Everyone is staring at me, but I look at only Emmett when I say this next part. "I realize that you hate me. You made that abundantly clear. That I'm not good enough for her. What you really think of me. But I will never be like my father. I will spend every day treating Del the way she deserves. I will take care of her and make her happy. And one day, I'll care for our children the way your parents did. Not the way my dad did. I want to be everything he wasn't for our family!" By the end of my speech, my voice had risen to a yell, so worked up with emotions.

Del has a soft hand resting on my thigh, and I cover it with my own, giving her hand a reassuring squeeze. Her touch is grounding, and her soft gaze makes my breathing come a little easier.

"I don't hate you, Hudson." Emmett is looking at me with unmistakable remorse.

I try not to scoff, but am unable to hold it in. I didn't hallucinate everything he said to me. "Listen, it's fine," I say dismissively. Del and I have said our peace, and I'm ready to leave whenever she is.

I look at her and we exchange a look that may seem like nothing to the rest of the table, but is enough for us to under-stand. I ask, *Are you ready to go?*

She quirks a brow and asks, *Hear him out?*

If that's what she wants, that's what she'll get.

I cant my head as an invitation for him to continue speaking, making it clear that I will not sit here longer than I have to.

He clears his throat and looks to his brothers for support. They both give him a nod, which gives him the courage he needs to speak. "I'm sorry for what I said. I didn't mean any of it."

He looks relieved when he finally gets the words out, but I only feel more anger. He didn't *mean it*. I have a hard time believing that. A person can't say those things if they haven't consciously thought them before.

I hold out a hand to make sure he stays quiet. "This goes for all of you," I look at all the men sitting across from me. "I will accept it if you don't like me. It's something I'll have to learn to live with. What I will not accept is you all acting like little dick swabs and making Del uncomfortable. You're her brothers, and she needs you all in her life. I will not give her up, so we need to find some way to coexist."

"None of us hate you," Beckett says calmly.

"We love you, Hudson. You're like a brother to us," Cash adds.

Emmett nods along to his brother's words. "You're my best friend," he says meekly. He almost sounds afraid that I'll reject him. "I love you and I don't want to lose you."

Hope blooms in my chest. They all still want me in their lives. I can have Del and my friends.

But, looking at Emmett now, I can still see the look of disgust on his face when he told me I'll end up exactly like my father.

I drop my gaze so I'm no longer looking at them. I don't want them to see how much they hurt me.

"You didn't tell me," Emmett breaks through the tense silence. My head rises until we're looking eye to eye.

"Tell you what?"

"About you and Lilah."

"We were going to. That night," I murmur.

"Fuck," he grumbles and drags a hand down his face.

I stare at him, dumbfounded. Is he upset that he didn't know?

"We're best friends, and you didn't tell me." And there's the confirmation I was looking for. He's hurt that I kept this from him, so he wanted to hurt me back.

"You know now," I say with a bit more punch than necessary. Just because he was hurt did not give him the right to hurt me and embarrass me in front of Del. An eye for an eye and all that.

"You have to admit, the way we found out was less than ideal," Cashton says, trying to break the tension.

I give him a dramatic eye roll. "Yes, the punch to my jaw did feel *less than ideal*," I say with a dramatized air quote.

He winces. "I'm sorry about that. I was just a little caught off guard."

"At least you don't think I'm trash," I say while turning my attention back towards Emmett.

"He doesn't think that, right, Em?" Del says, trying to keep the two of us civil.

Everything feels normal between Cash, Beck, and I now. Cash is back to his playful self and Beck is back to his *couldn't give a fuck less* self. But, Emmett and I are still tense.

"I never said you are trash," he says through gritted teeth. I don't understand his frustration.

"You might as well have."

He stands abruptly, sending his chair backwards. The loud bang makes Del jump, and I instinctively pull her closer to me.

"What the hell?" I ask, getting to my feet as well. We stand at about the same height, so we're looking each other in the eye from across the table.

"You didn't tell me!" He yells, pointing an angry finger at my chest. "I'm your best friend, and you didn't tell me you're in love with my sister!"

"Well, it was pretty obvious," Beck chides, looking smug.

"Shut up," we all say in unison.

"In that moment, when I saw you with her, I realized how long you had been lying to me. How much you kept from me. I wanted to hurt you the same way you hurt me. I know now that wasn't fair. You are good enough for Del, and I know you will always take care of her, but for a few minutes, I couldn't fathom why you would keep something like this from me."

Dels is on her feet and coming to my defense before I have a chance to respond. "Maybe he didn't tell you because you're all freaks and he knew you'd torment him about it. Kind of like how you teased me relentlessly for having a crush on him when we were kids."

"That's different, and you know it. We also teased you for saying the bear from that TV show we watched was husband material. We would have teased you about anyone. But, Hudson's our friend. I'm not mad you two are together, I'm actually happy for you. I just feel hurt that he didn't tell me."

He looks so tired.

I feel so tired.

We both just want this to be done.

"I should have gone to you. I should have told you it was all a lie, but I was... well, I was just ashamed."

At his admission, I breath easier. The air surrounding me feels comforting, rather than suffocating.

I have my friends back.

He didn't mean any of it. He was as devastated as I was.

I was worried that our entire friendship was a lie, but he was thinking the same thing. He thought I was keeping my true feelings and, essentially, who I was, a secret from him.

He watches me earnestly, waiting for me to say something.

Spur of the moment, brought on by my gratitude for his acceptance and forgiveness, I march around the table and throw my arms around him. I bury my head in the crook of his shoulder and bear hug him like we did as children. He hugs me back with equal conviction.

When we pull away, I give him a look that asks *We good?* He answers with a subtle nod of the head, which I know translates to *Yes, we're good.*

He gives me a brotherly slap on the shoulder. "I'm happy for you, but hurt her, and I'll have no choice but to hurt you back."

A deep rumbling laugh slips past my lips. I am overjoyed that he has the wherewithal to threaten me. It means everything is back to normal.

I step back and throw my arm around Del, shooting her a bright smile, trying to convey without words that everything is as it's meant to be.

Chapter Thirty-One

Delilah

What the hell is going on? One second, they're screaming at each other, and the next they're hugging like monkeys at the zoo.

Hudson's looking down at me with a glimmer in his eyes. I'm not even exaggerating. He's vibrating with a joy that should be infectious. The problem is, I have no idea what's going on.

Everything seems to be forgotten. Just like that.

All my brothers seem to be happy as they look at Hudson embracing me. Emmett has even sat down and started making a plate of hot dogs and potato salad.

In the distance, I hear a joke being tossed, then a rumble of laughter.

But I'm not sure if I can move on as easily as they are.

I'm not ready to forget the way they diminished Hudson and tried to manage my relationship.

"That's it?"

My voice sounds angry, but I don't know why. I'm relieved that Hudson has his friends back. That my brothers are accepting, even happy, that we are together.

I just feel like it can't be that easy.

Emmett points at my empty seat at the table, indicating that I should sit and grab a plate. "It's fine, Lilah." He looks at Hudson, "We're all good, right?"

"Everything's the way it should be," he answers and drops a soft kiss on top of my head.

A chorus of gagging noises envelops that air. "You can date but you are not allowed to do that shit around us," Cash states, as if it's a new law.

Hudson and I look at each other, speaking a thousand words without saying a single one. Then we laugh. "Not going to happen. I've waited a long time to get my hands on Del, I'm not wasting a single second of it."

"I think you two might actually kill me," Emmett says in a monotone voice, but the smirk tugging on his lips gives him away.

I want to hug everyone at this table and tell them all how much I love them.

Tonight gave me everything I could possibly want. The love of my life and my family. We are all so critically entwined that the idea of our group separating causes a sharp pang in my chest.

My emotions are rushing to the surface faster than I can regulate them. A choked sob escapes my lips, and everyone at the table freezes, turning all their attention on me.

I try to wipe the stray tears off my face, but Hudson's on me before I have the chance. His big hands frame my face as he looks me up and down critically, as if he's searching for anything that could be bringing me discomfort.

"What's wrong?" He sounds just short of frantic.

I feel bad for worrying him, but seeing the way he drops everything to check on me makes another wet sob bubble out of me.

The dark pools of his eyes get soft as he waits for me to speak. His thumbs trace soft, comforting circles on my cheekbones.

"I just... I don't know how to feel."

"About what, ladybug?"

After getting the last tear off my face, I take a deep breath and try to explain. "Everything with them," I wave in my brother's direction. "They were complete dickswabs to you, and they tried to take you away from me."

"We weren't trying to take him away from you, dumbass."

I ignore Cash and keep my focus on Hudson. When I look at him, I'm able to breathe easier. My problems and concerns seem more manageable when he's around.

Keeping a soft hold of my face, he angles my jaw until our eyes meet. "Nothing was ever going to keep me away from you." I feel like he's talking directly to my heart, because it flutters when he speaks. "And as far as what they said..." He trails off for a moment like he's not sure what to say. I know he's still hurt, but he's willing to forgive them for my sake. I don't want him to sacrifice his peace of mind for me.

I put my hand on his chest, cocooning his heart with my palm. It beats steadily, easing my thrumming pulse. "I don't want you just to ignore what they said. I know you'd do it for me, but I don't want you to. If they hurt you, I want them to grovel for your forgiveness."

"I've hated myself for weeks for the things I said to him!" Shame leaks out of Emmett's voice. "He's my brother, and I hurt him. I hate myself for that."

"Ladybug," Hudson whispers. "They are the only family I have ever known. I need to forgive them, and I hope in time you can too."

For him, I will.

I nod in understanding, then turn my attention to address my brothers. "Did you mean it?" Deep in my heart, I know they didn't. They all love Hudson as much as I do. I believe him when he says it's been killing him since it happened. Em feels emotions deeply but doesn't always know how to handle them.

"Of course I didn't mean it! I said the first thing I could think of to break up the situation. I was caught off guard and panicked. My brain said *fix it*, but it didn't know what needed fixing. It just said get Hudson away from Lilah." He takes a ragged breath, running his fingers through his hair and pulling on the ends. "Fuck, Hudson I'm so sorry. It's obvious how much you love her. I feel stupid for not putting the pieces together sooner."

"You should," Beck interjects in his usual unbothered tone. "Henely and I figured it out years ago."

Cash spins in his chair and dramatically asks, "Why didn't you tell me?"

322

"We wanted to see if it went anywhere without you messing it up."

He looks offended. "How would I mess it up?"

"Well, you're not exactly subtle." It's true, he's not. He's loud and proud about the things he thinks and feels.

"Dick," he mutters.

"I'm sorry I never told you guys, I just didn't want to lose you or her. I was willing to accept that I'd only ever be her friend as long as she was in my life."

Emmett and my brothers laugh. "And to think we were ever worried about this relationship," he says sarcastically. "He's always been wrapped around her finger." More laughing hits the air, and when I look to gauge Hudson's reaction, I see he's laughing too.

Seeing him comfortable, laughing freely with his friends, makes a smile break out across my face.

As if he feels my eyes on him, he looks over at me. His smile mirrors mine.

It feels right to be laughing and smiling with my entire family. Having everyone I love together is everything I've ever wanted.

"Stop looking at each other like that?" Cash groans like he's disgusted.

"Like what?" Hudson asks without taking his eyes off mine.

"Like you're going to kiss her," Emmett says with the same disgusted tone.

Hudson smirks, his lips curling into a pleased smile. "But I am going to kiss her." Then he leans in and kisses me softly, slowly. It's a chaste movement, but it says everything words cannot. That he loves me and will always love me.

A melody of groans and gagging noises flows in the background, and we break apart and start laughing. "Better get used to that, you'll be seeing it for the rest of your lives." Then he looks at me and whispers, "I promise."

Chapter Thirty-Two

Delilah

One Month Later

S pring has come and gone, inviting summer to take its place. The air is warm, lacking the cool breeze the spring offers, but instead giving us more hours of sunlight.

For someone like me who lives in Stone Lake, I take full advantage of the sunlight. Living this far north, we spend several months of the year in relative darkness. Not an hour of sunlight gets wasted in the summer.

I took a drive to town the other day, and on my way back, I saw the tell-tale signs of a strawberry bush in the ditch along the highway. Delicate white flowers, reminiscent of a fresh snowfall, decorated the slope off the road.

Hudson doesn't like it when I pick berries on the side of the road. He prefers the safety of the woods or the fields on the farm. He says it's not safe for me to be that close to traffic, especially since my mind tends to drift away from reality. Even now, when I go to the fields or woods, Hudson likes to be with me. He says it's because he wants to help and spend time with me, but I think it's his way of protecting me.

I've been protected my entire life by my four older brothers, but being protected by the man I love is different. It's a new kind of safety that soothes my soul.

Today, however, I reverted to my old ways. I couldn't drive past the strawberry patch any longer without stopping. Even from the road, I could tell that the berries were red as a fall apple and ripe from the summer sun.

I saddled up Izarra and hooked an old wooden wagon to her saddle. We've spent a lot of years together, so she's fully capable of hauling the wagon. It's not very big, and we go slowly through a clear field, just to be safe.

While I pick berries and throw them into my pails, Iz grazes on the mouth-watering green grass in the nearby field. She loves the freedom of the wind as it flows through her mane.

I dressed in a tank top and shorts, but the sun's rays are still penetrating my exposed skin. Sweat coats down my neck and back, but I can't stop now. These berries are the definition of perfection. I know it may sound strange, but they are. They are juicy and sweet, without a hint of bitterness. I may be a berry nerd, but I know exactly what makes the best kind of jam, and these berries are it.

Time has escaped me. It could have been minutes or hours since I've been out here, but I can't stop now. The sun is now on the opposite side of the sky from when I started, and a cool breeze chills the moisture on my skin.

Five large buckets are filled and loaded up in Iz's wagon, and I'm dragging one more to it now.

I jump on the wagon and brace myself as I lift the heavy bucket off the ground and onto the wooden surface. My knees quiver and my back aches as I use all my leftover strength to pull it over the final lip. I let out a whimper of pain on the last stretch of effort. I'm always sore after a day of picking, but I've definitely overdone it tonight.

Jumping off the wagon proves to be a mistake as my back twinges and I stumble to the ground. I stay on my knees, the cool dirt digging into my naked skin as I try to get my breathing under control.

In and out.

In and out.

My muscles spasm every time I take a breath.

I'm now conscious of just how low the sun is in the sky. If I don't get back home soon, Hudson will start to panic.

Over the last few weeks, he's moved his belongings into my house. It only makes sense, since he spends his days and nights there anyway.

I like having him in my home. *Our* home.

Seeing his big boots next to my smaller ones in the front entry, smelling his scent when I walk through the front door, waking up next to him every morning with his arms banding tightly around me. It feels like all the stars have finally aligned.

When I was living alone, I could do whatever I wanted, whenever I wanted. Now that I have someone looking after me, I need to be mindful of the time I spend away.

Before, I would have curled up in this field and stayed until morning. Now, I need to get back to my cowboy before he loses his mind.

Because he will.

He's turned into an even bigger protector since we became official.

Not that I'm complaining.

I love his protectiveness over me.

How am I going to get home to him in my condition? I can't even get off the ground.

Fuck.

If I have to call him for help, I'll never hear the end of it.

Succumbing to my fate, I start to dial him when hoof beats sound in the distance. Their rumble shaking the ground underneath me.

A silhouette of a broad man on a horse appears in front of me. I try to shield my eyes to see who it is, but the setting sun is blinding. It's not until his horse stops in front of me and blocks out the sun that I see who it is.

"Would it kill you to listen to me?" Hudson asks with a tinge of anger. Shit.

I look up at him from my knees. He looks like a god perched up so high on Lucky's back. "It might."

He tries to stop the grin from forming on his face and fails. "You're such a brat."

"But I'm your brat," I say with an overdramatic, flirtatious smile.

He jumps off his horse and crouches down in front of me, his elbows resting on his knees. He's lowered himself to my level, but he is still towering over me. "For the rest of your life."

I love it when he says things like that.

"Let's get you home. We have a big day tomorrow." He pushes back to his feet and holds a hand out for me to take.

There's a big farmers' market in town tomorrow, and I'll be running my own booth.

Hudson arranged for my brothers to help us set up my table and bring all the jams I have stored at home into town.

I stare up at his outstretched hand, but I don't take it.

He quirks his head at me in question. "We can camp out here another night, but I didn't bring any blankets. Come on, let's go home."

When I still don't take his hand, he bends at the waist and hauls me up from under my arms. The sudden movement fills my body with a burning pain. A shriek escapes my lips.

I wrap my legs around his waist and my arms around his neck, but he pulls his face from mine to look at me. His face is a mask of terror. "What happened, ladybug? Did I hurt you?" He frantically moves his hands over my body, and I gasp when he skates a palm over my lower back.

His eyes widen. "What happened?"

Embarrassed, I lower my eyes from his. "I was trying to lift the bucket into the cart."

He groans as if he's in pain. "Why didn't you tell me what you were doing? I would have come with you."

He's obviously figured out that I was, in fact, berry picking on the side of the road.

Not many ways to hide something like that, I suppose.

"How did you know I was out here?"

He starts walking me to our horses, his hands cradling me protectively. "Emmett came over to help me load your jams in the truck for tomorrow, and he said he saw you, and I quote, 'rolling around in the ditch.' I put the pieces together. Figured you went to the patch you've been rubbernecking every time we drive by."

Damnit.

I knew Emmett was coming over. He said he was stopping over tonight to help Hudson load the truck. If I hadn't lost track of time, I would've beaten him home, and nobody would have been any the wiser.

Well, I suppose the gallons of berries would have given me away.

Sheepishly, I raise my eyes to Hudson's soft brown ones. "Are you mad at me?"

I know he's not. I think he's physically unable to be mad at me, but he knows I don't like it when it happens on the rare occasions.

His eyes soften even further, taking on a dreamy expression. Yes! I've got him.

"I'm not mad at you, ladybug, I just don't like it when you come out here alone." I do feel bad for scaring him. All he wants to do is keep me happy and safe.

"Let's go home," I whisper, nuzzling my nose into his neck. He smells like the forest, strong and comforting.

He helps me take a seat in my saddle, and we start making our way home. We go slow to accommodate the wagon and my sore back. Every few minutes, I feel his gaze on me, making sure I'm still comfortable.

Truthfully, I'm in a lot of pain. I'm eager to get home and lie in bed. Curl up next to Hudson and have him stroke my hair until I fall asleep.

The sun has retired for the night by the time the porch lights come into view. When we stop in front of the barn, Hudson helps me dismount and guides me to take a seat on a rogue hay bale.

I watch as he untacks both of our horses and stalls them up for the night. Then, without me asking, he takes my buckets of berries and hauls them to the outbuilding where I store my merchandise.

By the time he's done, his skin has a sheen of sweat from the exertion, and mine has a layer of goosebumps from the breeze. He picks me up bridal style in his arms and carries me through the house and into our bedroom. The heat of his skin warms me as I bury my head in his chest.

Gently, he sets me on the edge of our bed and walks into the bathroom. I try to follow him, but my muscle twinges, and I let out a small moan. "Stay," he says, and disappears into the bathroom.

I hear him clinking around before I hear water start gushing out of the faucet. He's filling up the bathtub.

After a few more minutes, he comes back into the room. With no clothes on.

Yum.

"Quit oggling me," he teases, but I can see the heat dancing in his irises.

I dramatically look him up and down before biting my bottom lip between my teeth.

He groans, and I see his muscles tightening around his chest.

He walks up to me and drags his fingers over the waistline of my shorts, teasing the soft skin underneath. "I'm going to strip you naked and carry you into the bath. The heat will help your muscles."

Slowly, he raises my shirt over my head, kissing my neck, chest, and each of my nipples. A heat starts blooming in my lower belly as he unbuttons my shorts and carefully slides them down my legs.

I'm sitting in front of him in nothing but a pair of plain panties. He steps back to admire me, and I shiver under his gaze. "So beautiful," he rumbles under his breath, and I beam from his approval.

In contrast, his rough hands are so gentle. He slowly maneuvers my panties down my legs, leaving me completely bare in front of him.

He trails a hand down my body, starting at my neck, dragging his fingertips to my center. He gives me one feather-light touch before he pulls away.

Then, effortlessly, he carries me to the clawfoot tub and sets me into the warm water. My body relaxes instantly, and I can't stop the moan that slips out.

He stands outside the bath, looking down at me. I reach out my hand to him as an invitation.

I scoot forward as he steps inside the bath and lowers down behind me. One of his hands wraps around my waist and pulls me flush against him.

His muscular thighs act as a wall on either side of me and his stiff cock rests against my back.

I try to wiggle against him, hoping to tease him, but the movement hurts. He notices instantly and puts one of his big hands against my stomach, stilling my movements. "Stop moving, baby. Just relax and let me make you feel good."

By feel good, he means gently massaging my entire body. The longer I sit in the warm water while he kneads my muscles, the more the pain disappears.

My head is resting against his shoulder, and I'm pretty sure I doze off for a moment before his low whisper brings me back. "Are you feeling better?"

"Mhmm," I answer sleepily.

The hand he has resting against my stomach drifts lower and lower, igniting a spark inside me.

His palm rests over my mound, not touching, but holding almost protectively.

Testing my back, I grind against him and find the pain is almost completely gone, so I grind again. He keeps his hand loose enough that I don't get any friction, and I whine. "Please, Hudson."

"You need to relax," he coos. Instead of pulling away, he puts a grounding hand where my shoulder and neck meet. Then he dusts his fingers over my clit, so lightly I can only feel the ghost of his touch.

He is a torturer. I need more. "Help me relax, then. This is not relaxing."

Somehow, he's winding me higher and higher while barely touching me. He's only grazing me lightly, yet my clit is throbbing.

I feel my intimate wetness seeping out of me, but he doesn't increase the pressure. No matter how much I beg and whine, he barely touches me.

"Is this what you need, ladybug?" He finds my struggle humorous; I can hear it in his voice.

"I need more, and you know it," I growl.

"Like this?" He finally presses two of his fingers firmly on my clit and starts to make small circles.

My body reacts immediately, tingles spreading down my legs and twisting in my stomach.

I could come just from his first touch.

A few more spins around my bundle of nerves and I'll fall over the edge.

He gives me exactly what I need, tightening his circles and applying the perfect amount of pressure. All my muscles start to tighten as my control begins to dissipate. My body starts to quiver, and moans spill from my lips.

"That's my girl. Come for me."

I respond immediately, losing my control. My mind floats to a place I can only reach in Hudson's arms. My body trembles, but I still feel grounded as I push further into his embrace.

He rubs me softly as my orgasm subsides, and tightens his arm around me as I come down.

His lips pepper kisses on my face and neck. Down to my shoulder and back up.

I do my best to turn in his arms, but it's a tight squeeze in the tub. My knees dig into the porcelain wall, but I'm able to wrap my arms around his waist and rest my cheek against his chest.

"Don't get too comfy, I need to get you into bed."

I grumble even though I know he's right. I don't move to help him, but I don't fight as he stands and carries me to bed either. He pats me dry with the softest towel we have. Then, he covers me up with our quilt and climbs into bed next to me.

I throw my body over his and let the steady rhythm of his breathing lull me to sleep, feeling nothing but adoration for the man under me.

I've loved Hudson Owens for nearly twenty years. Our story started when we were children, before we knew the true meaning of love. But somehow, despite everything, we ended up exactly where we were meant to be.

Epilogue

Hudson

One Year Later

"Alright, what have we got?" Emmett sits at the breakfast table at the main house with a plat map of the property spread out in front of him.

"Right here," Cash points to an area in the southern field, "is full of them, *and* you can hear the river."

Emmett uses a red pen and circles the area, adding to the already marked-up map.

Beck nudges his way in front of the map and swipes the marker out of his hand. "Do it here," he says finally and puts a dot in the northernmost corner.

"Why there?" I ask. It has to be perfect, which is why we've been searching the property since the snow melted and the earth started to bloom.

We divided the property into four sections, and each of us took a zone.

"Because," he says dramatically. "The hill is covered with them, and on top of it, it has the best view of the sunset on the entire property."

"And you're sure they're there?" If they're not there, my plan won't work.

"Yes, I'm sure. Although I don't know why you're so obsessed with the weeds."

I roll my eyes. "They're not weeds; they're clovers."

Clovers have always been significant to Del and I. From the time we were children to adulthood, they were a way to keep us close.

Her brothers don't understand why they're so important and why I will not even consider proposing to Del in a spot without them.

When I asked them to help me find the perfect spot to pop the question, they were all excited to help. Even Beck graced me with one of his rare smiles. Then I told them I wanted it to be in a field of clovers, and they started to grumble.

They said she would say yes to me anywhere, and although that boosted my ego, I was insistent that it needed to be in a clover field.

So, they got to work searching the property. Every day when we had to check cattle in the fields, we looked for the perfect spot and marked it down. Then, at the beginning of the week, we reconvened and marked all possible locations on the big map I had printed out.

"Want to go check it out?" He offers.

I nod eagerly and let him lead me to the potential place where I'm going to ask Del to be my wife.

"What are we doing out here? We're going to be late for dinner?"

I asked Del to take the long way to her family's house, but I diverted from our regular route so we would end up on the top of the hill.

We rode our horse here, but I convinced her to stop and let them graze for a few minutes.

"I wanted to show you something." I've been trying to act calm, but I swear I can hear a quiver in my voice.

My body has been coated in a sheen of cold sweat since the moment I woke up, and in the last few hours, my stomach began to twist.

When I spoke to Emmett this morning, he told me I needed to get it together because I looked like I was going to faint. Not very helpful.

Who knew asking the love of your life to marry you would be this stressful? Her brothers say I have nothing to worry about, but I can't prevent it.

The only thing I've wanted for as long as I can remember is Del. She gave me the strength to stand up to my father and create the life I want for myself.

Her tiny hands take mine, and she rubs soft, soothing circles on my rough skin. "Hudson, what's wrong?" She takes a step closer and whispers, "You're shaking."

I look down and see that she's right. My hands are trembling in her still ones. I take a deep breath and close my eyes, willing myself to calm down.

When I open my eyes and see Dels looking up at me with wonder, my nerves settle.

I want to spend the rest of my life looking at those eyes. I want my children to have her eyes. I want it all with her.

"Look," I say, and direct her to stand in front of me so she's facing the setting sun. The sky is draped in an ombre of oranges and yellows, almost glowing with intensity.

"It's beautiful," she says with wonder in her voice.

I move fast and kneel behind her, digging the velvet box out of my pocket.

She turns around the second the box creaks open.

Her surprised gasps echo in the air as she looks down at me. "What are you doing?"

"Delilah Walton," I start, miraculously with a clear voice. "I have loved you for almost twenty years. The first day I met you, and you declared I would be your best friend, I knew I was in trouble. And I have been. I haven't met a single person besides you who ignites my soul. Who makes me want to be better. I want to spend the rest of my life loving you the way you deserve. Please, Del. Will you make me the luckiest man alive and marry me?"

As soon as the words come out, she's on top of me, tackling me to the ground with a hug. She holds me tight, and I squeeze her back. I never want to let her go. This is the moment I've been dreaming of since I learned the concept of marriage. She's the only one I want to love, cherish, and protect.

"Yes! Yes, I want to marry you!" She squeals with delight.

An overwhelming sense of relief and satisfaction takes root in my chest. She said yes. Delilah will be my wife. "You didn't even see the ring yet."

"Pshh, I don't care about that. I just want you."

I give her another squeeze before I put the ring box in front of her face. Her cheeks are flushed, and a glossy sheen is dancing in her eyes.

"Is that what I think it is?"

I got the ring custom-made for her about a month after we settled things with her family. As soon as we were back to the place we were before and I knew we were okay, I got started on the ring.

It's four teardrop emeralds with the tips meeting in the middle. It looks just like the four-leaf clover Del gave me that I have hanging in my truck. "I found one, and this time it's my turn to give it to you."

The tears that were gathered in her eyes spill over and trail down her cheeks, but her smile only grows.

"I love you so much, Hudson."

I slip the ring on her finger and feel nothing but satisfaction and gratitude. "I love you, Delilah." Then I kiss her. I kiss her for all the times I wanted to but never could. For all the times I will in our future.

She has made me the luckiest man alive. She is luck to me.

.

www.ingramcontent.com/pod-product-compliance
Lightning Source LLC
Chambersburg PA
CBHW070911260626

47162CB00007B/2634